KU-111-915

25/-
30p.

HEARTS OF STONE

EDWARD TAYLOR

HEARTS
OF
STONE

JOHNSON

LONDON

© Edward Taylor 1968

*All characters in this story are fictitious and are not intended
as reference to any living person*

First Published 1968
S.B.N. 85307 011 3

Printed in Great Britain by Thomas Nelson (Printers) Ltd.
London and Edinburgh

FOR JOHNSON PUBLICATIONS LTD.
11-14 STANHOPE MEWS WEST, LONDON S.W. 7

To My Mother

AUTHOR'S PREFACE

I WRITE this Preface primarily to impress upon the reader that the book was not written entirely as a comedy—although I hope that its pages will raise the odd chuckle. Nor do I believe that the hero (if such is a wholly appropriate description) would necessarily be entirely out of place were he to appear in the hallowed Palace of Westminster tomorrow.

Going round the country, I get the impression that the average elector does not hold Members of Parliament in the highest regard. 'The only qualifications for being an M.P. are that you mustn't be a Peer, a lunatic or a convicted criminal,' one cynic recently advised me, 'and although this offers a very wide choice it's amazing how one or two of each of these categories slips through from time to time!'

The book is designed primarily to remove this false impression. My experience has been that even the M.P.s with the worst possible public images are required to work the most unreasonable hours in the most unreasonable conditions. And it is sad that the minority of M.P.s with the gift of catching the headlines often give the impression by their reported activities that the other Members are a shiftless and lazy

crowd. On any fair piecework assessment, I think that
the British public get fair value in effort and hard
slogging from their representatives. Whether the result
of their hard work is all that it might be is another
question—and here we come to the dreaded question
of 'the system' which I have endeavoured to touch
upon in *Hearts of Stone*.

I also deal with the frustrations of the job. The
voicing of any view on any subject by an M.P. invariably brings furious criticism from some section of the
electorate. And the voicing of none brings universal
condemnation.

A further frustration is that those with the courage
and conviction to stick their necks out in calling for
action on any cause find it almost a superhuman task
to translate, through the Parliamentary system, their
views into legislative action. The mountainous scrap-
heap of discarded Private Members' Bills is an ever-
present memorial to this sad fact.

But I think that the one message which must be
conveyed by those who have been lucky enough to be
in Parliament is the sheer fascination of the place. 'It's
like drink to an alcoholic,' I was told by an 'old-timer'
when I arrived. 'You don't enjoy it at the time, but
you miss it terribly when the supply is cut off!' The
pitiful spectacle of M.P.s who have lost their seats or
resigned and who thereafter wander through life rather
like dispirited canines deprived of their favourite bone
bears testimony to the fascination of the Mother of
Parliaments.

It has been great fun for me to write *Hearts of Stone*

because it provided an opportunity to get the frustrations of three years at Westminster out of my system.

Could I perhaps take the opportunity to thank the delightful and talented Miss Rosemary Meynell who waded so conscientiously through the text to purge it of the split infinitives and other grammatical outrages with which Parliamentary debating infects us. I must also thank Dr Donald Johnson, that rumbustious and fearless publisher, ex-M.P. for Carlisle, who has so generously taken the gamble to sponsor my first novel.

TEDDY TAYLOR

WESTMINSTER
S.W.1

"take away our hearts o' stone,
and give us hearts o' flesh"

Sean O'Casey: JUNO AND THE PAYCOCK, ACT III

HEARTS OF STONE

AS Mr Gibley Horn, M.P., tramped through the 'Noes' Lobby for the fifth time that Thursday evening, he wished that he had never heard of the Spotted Hummerfly. Only the previous Friday he had appealed to his Parliamentary colleagues to take the necessary legislative steps to protect the insect from the extinction with which it was threatened by modern chemical insecticides. But now he would gladly have seen the last few million survivors subjected to all the tortures and indignities which twentieth - century science could inflict on the wretched creatures. And, in his gloomy frame of mind, he might even have wished the same fate on Miss Avril Phillimore and the whole Executive Committee of the Insect Friendship League who had landed him in this mess.

Gibley's deep despondency was not confined secretly in his heart. It was there for all to see. The podgy round head which supported his bald and shining scalp drooped forward more than usual and his agitated shuffling and pushing through the mass of Tories, crammed into the Lobby, signified more a wish to get away from the jollity and chatter of the throng than an anxiety to record his opposition to Amendment 231 of the Land Drainage Bill, which had just been so tediously and technically discussed in the House of Commons Chamber.

Jimmy Winterton, who had attained the reputation of being one of the most popular and sincere Members by consistently congratulating all and sundry on even the most mediocre speeches, and humbly seeking their advice on non-controversial matters with a reserve and appreciation more appropriate to the Delphic Oracle, saw immediately that in Gibley Horn there was a candidate ripe for his special brand of concern and consolation. He elbowed his way through the throng, pausing briefly to offer good cheer to a new Norfolk M.P. whose name he could not recall.

'Splendid speech tonight, old boy! You're *so* right about these new powers being a threat to the liberty of the individual.'

Having thoroughly convinced his now-beaming East Anglian colleague that his hesitant and dreary speech had been a great success and, incidentally, having made a new friend, he sidled up to Mr Horn.

'Gibley, my dear chap,' he began with enthusiasm, 'I've just been reading your Friday speech in *Hansard*. Of course, I read all the Reports at the week-end,' he added, truthfully and hurriedly, lest the original white lie would become apparent under cross-examination.

'You were quite magnificent and so right about the dreadful dangers of all this chemical stuff. These scientists will have us dead, or two-headed before we know where we are if we don't watch out. I'm terribly sorry that you had so little support on Friday—I had to be in my Constituency—but, a hundred years from now, they might realise how right you were,' he added, as though the plaudits of historians were adequate consolation for opposition and ridicule today.

Gibley's nod of recognition to Jimmy Winterton revealed that even in his sullen state he was not completely immune to praise and flattery, but his wound was deep and he said, quietly:

'I could have done with your support. Thought you might have been there. I only had seven with me in the Lobby.'

'I'm sorry, old chap, I just had to go to the Constituency. Some women's rally; but I never dreamt, for a minute, that you would be so deserted. My local N.F.U. man wrote to me about your Bill and I told him, quite bluntly, that I held you in the highest regard and knew that you would have good reasons for doing what you did.'

If he had been completely truthful, he would have also mentioned that his letter to the local N.F.U. man had ended with the unambiguous words, 'I shall certainly not support any Bill which could damage the interests of British Agriculture which renders such a splendid service to the community.' But the circumstances were hardly auspicious to publicise this part of his letter.

Having dipped lavishly into his bountiful store of goodwill, Jimmy Winterton moved up the Lobby where the tall, thin figure of Reggie Flowers, the recently appointed Minister of Labour, was temporarily isolated.

'Excuse me, Minister,' Jimmy whispered reverently,

'but I should greatly value your advice on a strike problem in my Constituency . . .'

Back, down the Lobby, Gibley Horn was a little cheered by Winterton's comments, but no praise, however generous, could wipe out the humiliatoin of Friday or its disastrous consequences. Nor could the pleasant and pleasing patter of his 350 colleagues in the Lobby eradicate the cold fact that 120 of these smiling faces had gone through the Lobby against *his* Bill on Friday; only seven had voiced their support for it, and more than two hundred had simply not been there when the roll had been called on the Spotted Hummerfly Protection Bill. It was a sobering thought.

*** *** ***

It was now a month or so since the day early in November of the previous year, soon after the reassembly of Parliament, when the name of Gibley Horn had been taken third out of the Clerk's box indicating that he had been successful in the Private Member's Ballot for the first time in his ten years as M.P. for Rossford. He had seen this immediately as a heaven-sent and timely opportunity to persuade the 55,000 Rossford electors that their Member of Parliament was active, impressive and statesmanlike. It might even, he mused, perhaps strike the spark which would fire off a new series of overdue and important legal reforms.

For here was a chance to present a Private Member's Bill on any subject and an opportunity to go down in history as the originator of a great new law, if only he could persuade his fellow M.P.s to support whatever noble cause he chose to champion.

Immediately he had telephoned Rossford 2495 and passed on the glad tidings to Alec Anderson, the full-time Conservative Party Agent, so that the news could be blazed across the local *Rossford Gazette*. And, accordingly, that week on page three (the front-page splash being taken up by some miserable bank robbery in High Street) could be seen the austere and dignified face of Gibley Horn, as it had been in the photographer's studio some twelve years ago, with the headline 'MR HORN M.P. LUCKY IN BILL DRAW'. Below there was the splendidly mysterious sub-heading 'CAUSE HE WILL CHAMPION STILL IN DOUBT'

The next week brought the first batch of suggestions as to what the cause should be. First there was a spate of letters in the post suggesting a variety of possibilities, including Bills to legalise the practices of assorted sexual perverts, Bills to provide semi-professional registration for plumbers and blacksmiths, Bills to give more power to Local Authorities, and Bills designed to take most of the existing powers away. Bills to simplify accountancy procedures which were themselves incomprehensible and Bills to repeal navigation laws passed in the reign of Elizabeth I.

And then came the week-end phone calls from constituents and others to his home in Rossford.

'Strange how your constituents always seem to get their inspiration at mealtimes,' his wife, Margaret, had

said with a sad uncomplaining shrug of her thin
shoulders, as she put Saturday's lunch back into the
oven for the third time. Poor Margaret! Interrupted
meals were part of the normal pattern of her life. She
had been a pretty woman once, with ideas and
ambitions of her own. Now, she was a faded shadow of
her former self, still faithfully trying to support her
husband, but worn down by the hardness of her lonely
lot and the hopelessness of trying to preserve a remnant
of ordinary family life.

The first telephone call had been from an hysterical-
sounding Blackpool man who urged that a Bill be
presented to ensure that he would get the legacy which,
he declared, his grasping cousin had stolen from him
thirty years ago 'with the connivance of the Police, the
Judges and the House of Lords'.

'Abolish pop singers' fees,' suggested another caller.
And a Scottish Sunday paper proposed, in fiery language, that any Scottish M.P. refusing to use a Private
Member's Bill to abolish local rates was unworthy of
the continued support of his constituents.

Gibley studied this series of suggestions with great
care and felt, for the first time since a rapturous crowd
in the Burgh Square had greeted the news of his
election, that the eyes of the nation were upon him.

But when he raised the subject in the Commons
Smoking Room the following week, he was over-
whelmed by M.P.s who offered to assist in Bills which
they themselves had unsuccessfully promoted in previous years.

Even Billy Greaves, the 'Private Bill King' from the

Labour side, stopped him in the Lobby to suggest a good cause with his usual urgent and alarming torrent of verbosity. Billy was always promoting 'Ten Minute Rule' Bills which never ceased to shock and never failed to disappear for ever in the maw of the Parliamentary machine. Gibley listened attentively, just in case Billy had stumbled on a good one, for once, that could attract all-Party support and favourable comment in the constituencies. But his attentive patience soon disappeared when Gibley identified the 'Cause of Today' through the tangle of Billy Greaves' agitated outpourings and he found reason to break off the interview. Greaves must have been joking, he thought.

What would the electors of Rossford have thought of their worthy Member promoting the Unmarried Mothers' Special Assistance Bill? He could imagine Mrs Cole-Pratt, his Conservative Ladies of Rossford Convener, glowering at him as though all the sin and promiscuity of the nation stemmed directly from his Private Member's Bill.

But every cause seemed to have its disadvantages. Alec Anderson, the Agent, stopped a few. Stricter lorry checks? The local haulage boys were not enthusiastic. Flood control? The local council was lukewarm, seeing in the proposal a vast increase in rating expenditure. House buyers' protection? 'All right for the house owners,' Alec explained, 'but does nothing for the Council tenants. We need more votes there. Remember, the shouts at the election meetings in the Glenby area that you didn't care a damn about them.'

'Get something for the housewives,' was Alec's sober

advice. 'Or something nice about children or dogs.'
But a feverish search proved beyond a shadow of a
doubt that most of the more obvious 'nice' bills about
housewives, children, dogs, budgerigars and other such
worthy sections of the community had been flogged to
death in decades of Private Bills.

A sudden inspiration to promote a Bill exempting
the churches from rates had sent Gibley scurrying
round enthusiastically to a local clergyman, only to
hear, to his surprise and embarrassment, that they had
always been exempt. The Minister's parting question,
'How long have you been our M.P., Mr Horn?' had
inferred discreetly that, in the Rev. Emmanual Gibb's
opinion, ten years was quite long enough for an M.P.
of average intelligence to ascertain the basic facts about
rating law.

The only gleam of hope came from a visit one
Sunday afternoon from Miss Avril Phillimore who
announced herself as General Director of the Insect
Friendship League.

She was a small waspish-looking lady, reminiscent
of an insect herself, dressed in old-fashioned rather
glittering clothes which might have found buyers in
the Chelsea Antique Market. Her jet black hair
was gathered into a most unbecoming bun at the
back, with wisps in front that reminded him of
antennae.

Gibley found her waiting for him at 'Beechgrove',
his home in the constituency, after she had been shown
into the cold, high-ceilinged drawing-room by Margaret. In the pretentious but uncomfortable setting of

the Horns' home, with its dowdy mock-antique furniture and frayed carpets, Miss Phillimore had seemed quite at ease. There had been cockroaches in the gloomy stone-flagged passages when they had first taken the house, and it crossed his mind that she, at least, would have appreciated them.

For half an hour she discoursed eloquently about the dangers and absurdities of chemical insecticides. And, every few minutes, she handed him Press cuttings reporting the views of scientists and doctors, of apparent standing, to the effect that some insecticides were intensely dangerous and were threatening the survival of the human race either by mass poisoning or by the more insidious process of causing sterility.

'Five per cent more grain production this year,' she exclaimed with a flourish, 'in exchange for the mass destruction of the human race this century!

'Is this the kind of bargain which the British housewife wants?

Gibley had to admit that, if such a proposition was put to the housewives of Rossford, there would be little doubt about their reply.

It seemed, from the good lady's argument, that there was a conspiracy of silence on the part of the Government which, like all its predecessors, was plagued with a balance of payments problem. To abolish insecticides would mean a steep rise in food imports and the extra bill might well turn the present problem into a crisis. Miss Phillimore sympathised with the Government. As a lifelong Conservative, she sympathised particularly with the present one. But a firm stand against mass poisoning would inspire the British people and make them willing to undertake greater sacrifices.

'Churchill or Disraeli would have seen the challenge immediately; and I am sure that Sir Oliver will see the issue if only it can be forcibly stated in the House of Commons. It will become the greatest political issue of the day!' Miss Phillimore claimed with confidence.

'The Socialists will be finished for ever if they oppose you . . . and you, Mr Horn, have a glorious opportunity to light a fire which will sweep through the nation.'

Having exhausted her powers of oratory, Miss Phillimore went on to explain the Insect Friendship League, its composition and its objective. Some people might think that they were cranks, she admitted, but the Executive Committee was chaired by an eminent professor and included company directors, a peer, business-men and ordinary housewives. It was supported entirely by voluntary subscriptions and, last year, more than £10,000 had been spent on literature, meetings and other forms of propaganda. The offices were in Cromwell Place in Birmingham, which had been chosen with a view to harnessing the support of the great industrial giants of the nation.

At an emergency meeting of the Executive, Miss Phillimore had been charged with the task of going to Rossford and ascertaining whether Mr Horn was a man with the courage, statesmanship and integrity to present the League's case.

'I am now convinced, Mr Horn,' she concluded, leaning forward to give weight to her words.

'Will you take on the battle?'

Gibley Horn could not hide the fact that he was impressed at the thought of leading a national campaign which would wipe out the Socialist Party, save humanity and put himself in the role of prophet and visionary, but a caution and reserve cultivated over the years made him hesitate.

'What kind of Bill had your League in mind and who would draft it?' he asked.

'No problem at all,' came the immediate response. 'The League has obtained expert advice and the Bill will be so well drafted that not even the Solicitor-General could take exception to it on legal grounds.' Miss Phillimore's voice took on conspiratorial overtones as she continued:

'We think that it would be best to spotlight the problem by concentrating on one particular chemical and one particular insect. To be precise—BX20 and the Spotted Hummerfly.'

'BX20,' she explained, fluttering her hands as she spoke, 'is a new chemical which is in almost every insecticide used in cornfields. We have had the most alarming reports from Paraguay about the effect on the health of people who have eaten bread made from corn sprayed with BX20 insecticides over a few years. It seems that the big American companies experimented with the new chemical in Paraguay and, so far, it has not yet been used in the U.S.A. The dangers must be all too obvious when the Americans refuse to have their own people poisoned, but why are the British Government doing nothing about it?' she demanded

'And where does the Spotted Humber come into this?' Gibley inquired, somewhat baffled.

'Hummerfly,' Miss Phillimore corrected him.

'These poor defenceless insects are being exterminated by BX20. It is quite horrible: they are found only in cornfields and millions of the little creatures have been wiped out.'

'It is not as if they do any harm at all,' she continued. 'If they spread malaria or something like that we would understand, but to go ahead, blindly, upsetting the balance of nature is quite criminal!'

'Our Chairman, Professor Himmelstein, is one of the world's top authorities on insects and he is quite convinced that to exterminate the Hummerfly with BX20 will have the effect of gradually poisoning whole populations within fifty years. So the Bill would be the *Hummerfly Protection Bill*; we could try to ban BX20 by Act of Parliament, but the lawyers assure us that the easiest way to do this is to give protection to the Hummerfly and this will have the effect of virtually banning the use of this dangerous chemical.'

She put on her spectacles, rummaged through a brief-case packed with papers, and produced a typed booklet which she presented to Gibley with a flourish.

'Here, Mr Horn, is the Bill.'

At the front was the title—The Spotted Hummerfly Protection Bill, and on page one the explanation that it was a Bill to prohibit the use of chemical insecticides designed to exterminate or resulting in the extermination of the insect commonly known as the Spotted Hummerfly.

'Be it enacted by the Queen's most Excellent Majesty,' the text continued, 'by and with the advice and consent of the Lords Spiritual and Temporal, and Commons, in this present Parliament assembled, and by authority of the same . . .'.

This looked like the real thing and, at least, Gibley thought, they couldn't turn this down simply on the grounds that it was badly drafted.

And there, on the back of the draft Bill, was the acknowledgment that it was 'Presented by Mr Gibley Horn and supported by . . .'

'Do you think that I could get many supporters?' Gibley asked doubtfully.

'Of course! Mr John Knox-Crichton is one of our League's patrons and he is a *very* prominent Conservative M.P. Then we have had letters of support from Mr Bothwell, the Labour M.P. for Darnley South and from that nice new Liberal M.P., Mr Forbes; and I'm sure many others would support a Bill presented by your good self, Mr Horn.'

'Well, I have a few friends,' Gibley admitted modestly, 'but this is something rather out of the ordinary.'

The conversation had gone on for twenty minutes and at that point the door of the drawing-room was quietly opened and Margaret Horn stepped into the room casting a rather wary eye at Miss Phillimore.

'I hope you're not forgetting your meeting with the Colonel at four this afternoon?' she queried. 'It's after half-past three already.'

There was, of course, no meeting at four and the

Colonel was mythical, but Mrs Horn traditionally used this useful military gentleman to help her husband break off unduly long interviews with the many callers at 'Beechgrove'. Her assessment of Miss Phillimore was clearly not of the highest, as the call to the Colonel had been announced after only twenty minutes compared with the normal half-hour she allowed for local callers.

Gibley responded at once:

'Of course, my dear, thank you for reminding me. I do hope you will understand, Miss Phillimore. I shall study the Bill carefully and get in touch soon.'

Anxious not to miss an opportunity, Miss Phillimore addressed Mrs Horn, as she rose to leave.

'Your husband and I have been having a conversation about chemical insecticides, Mrs Horn. What do the housewives you come in contact with think about all these new chemicals used in our food these days?'

Margaret Horn hesitated. Years of experience had taught her the wisdom of having no definite views on subjects which were even remotely political. But she saw no hidden dangers in offering her opinion on this.

'I think that there are far too many chemicals used these days. Food is so tasteless. It seems to me that the scientists are going too far.' She spoke with unaccustomed confidence.

'How *right* you are,' said Miss Phillimore and, turning triumphantly to Gibley, she exclaimed, 'I see that I have a strong ally in your wife, Mr Horn. I am sure that her views are those of housewives everywhere.'

Gibley Horn was impressed with his wife's immediate reaction and, as he ushered Miss Phillimore out, he wondered if this might not prove to be a splendid cause to champion.

'Something nice for the housewives,' Alec Anderson had suggested.

Here it was, on a plate!

❋❋❋　　❋❋❋　　❋❋❋

That evening, as he packed his case ready for the sleeper journey to London, Gibley pondered over Miss Phillimore's visit and her proposal. The more he thought of it, the better it seemed. Hardly anybody in Rossford would be antagonised by the Bill. Perhaps one or two of the few remaining farmers in the constituency might not relish it but they would soon be eliminated themselves as the advance of housebuilding went on round the Burgh into the neighbouring County. However, he could always have a word with the farming boys at Westminster to make sure.

And, if the housewives did feel strongly about this chemical stuff, he could get a great deal of support. Some of the Sunday papers, which were always dramatising new scandals, might jump at this one. 'GERM WARFARE IN YOUR HIGH STREET— ROSSFORD M.P. TO ACT'—he could picture the headlines already.

Before leaving for Glasgow, he phoned up Alec Anderson at his home to sound him out. The Agent responded immediately to the point about chemicals in food.

'The wife is always talking about that,' he admitted,

'I think the whole business is a nonsense fanned by the Press; but the important thing is that housewives *do* seem to care. Mind you, I wouldn't take this tasteless food lark too seriously—Clara's would be tasteless with or without this BX20 stuff.'

He paused to exchange jocular insults with his wife whose protests could be heard in the background.

'However, I don't fancy this title. Nobody's heard of the Hummerfly. Couldn't you call it the Housewives Protection Bill or the Pure Food Bill or something like that?'

'I'll see what the Whips Office say,' Gibley promised, 'but you like the idea anyway, Alec?'

'Not bad at all,' came the enthusiastic response. 'Have a nice week at the House and try to say something that I can boost up in the *Gazette*. Some people feel that you don't *talk* enough these days.'

'They should know better,' complained the M.P. 'It isn't easy beating 629 others to the mark—and most of them bletherers. Much of the important work is done in the Committees where the Press don't report.'

'You don't have to persuade *me*, old chap. It's the 30,000 readers of the *Gazette* I'm worried about: and don't forget to write to the F.O. about Mrs Bloomsbury's views on the Albanian frontier question. She's got a sister in Greece and is terrified about a war there —it might force her sister to come home.'

'I shall tell the F.O. that, if Mrs Bloomsbury's sister is as much of an objectionable old trout as Mrs Bloomsbury, then the Albanians are crazy to have any interest in Greece at all,' responded Gibley, by now in jocular form.

'And lose us fifty quid subscription? That's worth twenty letters to the Foreign Secretary!'

'You really should not say things like that about Mrs Bloomsbury over the phone,' Margaret suggested anxiously after Gibley had put the receiver down. 'You never know who might be listening. I'm always getting crossed lines these days.'

'Some day, Margaret dear, when we have enough fifty quids in the coffers of the Rossford Conservative Association, I shall not hesitate to tell the whole world what I think of Mrs Bloomsbury and her wretched sister!'

He picked up his case from the hall floor and gave his wife an affectionate kiss.

'Must fly now, dear, the train leaves at eleven. Back on Friday morning, same as usual! God and British Railways permitting,' he added as an afterthought.

'Why do you always have to go down on Sunday night, Gibley?' Margaret sounded querulous. 'Jerry Macdonald's wife says that he never leaves for London until Tuesday morning.'

'Yes, but look at Jerry's wife.' Gibley spoke without thinking and instantly wished he could eat his words. For Jerry's wife, ten years or so younger than Jerry, was a bit of a bombshell by M.P.'s wives' standards. She was always extravagantly dressed, in the height of fashion, and her 'top person' mannerisms and graceful carriage charmed the Scottish Tory ladies enough to make her their top pin-up girl. There were few constituencies which had not organised bazaars to be opened by Mrs Julia Macdonald and few voluntary organisations which had not approached her to grace their Garden Fêtes with her presence.

Julia would not, therefore, have had much chance of success in a popularity poll among other M.P.'s wives: Gibley still remembered his wife's depression when she found out that her invitation to open the Rossford Fête had only come after Mrs Julia Macdonald and three other ladies had replied that they could not be in Rossford on the appointed day.

'Seriously, my dear, I wouldn't have that woman as a cook! I've got the very best wife in the business,' he added, hastily, to compensate for the gaffe.

'The only reason I have to go down for Mondays is in case anything comes up in the House about Rossford County. I've got four Socialists surrounding me here and, if I am not there, they invariably make a point of mentioning it in their speeches, and then the *Gazette* is on to it like a shot. It's different for Jerry Macdonald with his 14,000 majority and two of the other three seats in his county held by Tories.'

There were, of course, other reasons for Gibley's early start to the week in London. Unable to afford a secretary, like most M.P.s, he had to rely on a girl from the Parliamentary agency and Monday mornings was an easy time to get a typist from there. On other days it was almost impossible. In addition he was forced to travel by train overnight rather than by air for economic reasons. If he parked his car at the Airport for the week, there would be little change out of £2, whereas he could leave his car by the Central Station, Glasgow, in the private car park owned by his constituency Chairman's business. The only recompense for this was a bottle of whisky at Christmas plus an occasional invitation to dinner at 'Beechgrove' to Major Perkins and his good lady. There was also the question of taxis at the London end. The short journey to his London hotel cost only 3/- from Euston, but around 14/- from the West London Air Terminal.

In short, the reason was money. A problem simply not considered by the said Mr Jerry Macdonald with his fourteen directorships and his estates, Gibley ruminated bitterly.

His extended farewells to Margaret had made him late for the train and his face was clouded as he drove out of the garage knowing that his normal forty-five-minute drive would have to be done in forty. Now that he was past his middle fifties, he did not like hurrying, especially in his car. The traffic always seemed to be worse when he was late and the automatic lights leagued together to frustrate his progress. Nasty pains in his chest came more often nowadays. He wondered if this was a serious sign or just indigestion. He realised he should consult his doctor but he knew that this would worry Margaret. He would have to check up with some London chap, but there was so little time and, anyway, doctors charged so much when they put up their plates at London addresses.

A perfect job, for that Prices' Board thing that the Socialists used to have when they were in power, he thought as he sped along the Glasgow road. The Board had disappeared under the heavy axemanship of the Tory Government when they took over after the

Labour Government had collapsed. Wonder what happened to all the Civil Servants? he mused aimlessly. No doubt sitting pretty in the Ministry of Agriculture by now.

Money, money, money, this was always his trouble. It seemed ridiculous when you looked at his income: £65 per week as an M.P. and another £500 a year from one solitary directorship in a distillery. The Littleglen Distillery had always had an M.P. on the Board and he had obtained the vacancy when old Colonel McAngus had been called to even higher places than the Distillery Board Room. Gibley had never been able to discover why they always took on an M.P. Perhaps, just to have the name in the Annual Report. Anyway, the £500 was very welcome.

But despite the income, he now had an overdraft of £400 in place of the tidy balance of £600 he had possessed when he had been elected. Where did the money go? That was the question. Time after time he had totted up an ideal balance sheet showing that he should have plenty to spare at the end of each month. But it never worked out that way. There was always some special expenditure which knocked out the calculations, and paying London hotel bills as well as keeping up his Rossford home was a constant drain.

'Beechgrove' involved the expenditure which tipped the balance. When he had bought the villa at the depth of the recession in '66, or was it '67? it had seemed a snip at £6,250. But, since then, he must have spent at least £500 a year on it. First, there was a bit of dry rot to cut out. Then there was the rewiring job. Then the house had to be repainted. The cost had been an exorbitant £342, but 'rich' M.P.s were not expected to complain about bills, especially if the contractors worked in the constituency. If he had got an outside firm to do the job, he would have had the permanent hostility of the local painters and, perhaps, the local Chamber of Commerce to contend with.

What an empty shell 'Beechgrove' seemed, now that their son, Keith, was studying at Yale and daughter, Joanna, married and living in Chester. Originally, the objective had been a bit of privacy which the old terrace house where they had been living previously could not provide. And 'Beechgrove', with its high garden wall and half-acre of ground, had seemed ideal. But it was now a pretty miserable place for Margaret to be left alone in for the whole week, even with Mrs Lawrence calling in each day to do some housework.

If only Joanna lived nearer home, his thoughts ran on. When she had married Michael, Gibley and Margaret had hoped that the boy could get a job in Glasgow or at least somewhere in Scotland. But the talk at that time of the possibility of a transfer had never come to anything and, last year, they had seen the couple only twice—once at Christmas and once when they had motored down for a week.

And poor Joanna had looked rather unhappy that time. Michael was a decent chap but always staying late at the office. He would certainly 'get places', that boy, but his poor young wife hardly saw him.

There were no children yet, and that was a shame because all the other bungalows round Joanna's home seemed to have a pram outside the door, while all that poor Joanna had was that funny little gnome with the pipe which she had insisted on taking away with her from 'Beechgrove' to place in the centre of her new home's lawn.

What an ordeal the wedding had been! £600 it had cost him with 350 guests invited. And even then there were many who were clearly hurt or outraged that they had not been included. It had, however, been a happy occasion marred only by the Press coverage. Unaccustomed to the reverence with which political figures have to treat the Press, Michael had very gallantly punched a photographer who was endeavouring to take a snap of Joanna in the undignified pose of extracting part of her wedding veil from a rosebush in front of the church. The result had been a poor photo in the *Daily Star* with the unfortunate caption of 'SHAMBLES AT SOCIETY WEDDING—GROOM IN PUNCH-UP'.

Altogether, the Rossford M.P. had not been too lucky with the Press in his Parliamentary career. Even when reporting his maiden speech, a time for generosity if there ever was one, the *Star* had recorded only the fact that he had sneezed twelve times while delivering it.

However, as his car raced down the Springburn Road towards the City Centre, Gibley Horn thought to himself that maybe these days of Press hostility were coming to an end. Properly presented, his Private Bill could be splash headline material for days, with no chance of a boomerang.

As he arrived at the car park, he realised to his astonishment that he had completed the journey in record time and could make his way leisurely to the station. There would be no time for his usual brandy in the Railway Hotel, but he could have one on the train.

Out of a sense of political loyalty to free enterprise, he had always supported the railway hotels ever since they had been denationalised, a splendid move by the Government shortly after they came to power. £200 millions extra for sensible capital development of the railways, and the shareholders of the new Railroad Hotel Company had done well also. The shares, issued at 25/-, were now 39/-, and still rising. This move had been a little compensation for those Tories who had objected to Sir Oliver's blunt refusal to go for straightforward denationalisation of the steel industry. Instead, he had allowed a 49 per cent public holding in five regional steel groupings, with the State retaining 51 per cent in each case. He had pointed out that this might satisfy the Labour Party if they ever got back to power.

'We must plan for even the most unlikely eventuality,' Sir Oliver had told the 1922 Committee of backbenchers, amidst laughter, 'and take the industry out of the political battlefield.' But, even now, the Socialists were still shouting for 100 per cent ownership and control by the State and for the evolution of 'industrial democracy' in steel, whatever that might mean.

Would they never learn?

2

As he approached the platform, Gibley saw by the bookstall the small and wizened figure of Peter McGarrity, the Labour Member for Glasgow, George Square. He was a friendly, cheery chap and Gibley looked forward to having a drink with him. Perhaps he might even sound him out on the Hummerfly Bill.

Peter was one of the seven Labour M.P.s for Glasgow, the Tories having, unexpectedly, gained six after the redistribution of the boundaries in a strange General Election where the Scottish Nationalists had received one vote in six in the city and almost captured a seat.

Most of the other Glasgow Labour M.P.s kept very much to themselves and did not speak a great deal to the Tory Members from the Counties. But Peter McGarrity was a friendly type who seemed just as happy in the company of the 'countiest' Tory as with Welsh miner Socialists.

'Good week-end, Pete?' Gibley inquired. 'McGarrity Towers in good shape?'

'Not bad,' Pete replied in a broad Glasgow accent. 'But the ceiling fell in on Sunday. It must be this Tory Government. Ever tried tomato soup à la plaster?'

'No, we don't serve that at Horn Court but I'll treat you to a brandy à la British Rail. What about it?'

'You're on. Let's go, before the price goes up again.'

The pair strode off towards the *Flying Claymore* and, as they approached it, they saw the hunched figure of Michael Walkinshaw scurrying up the platform.

'Bloody bomb thrower,' Pete growled, showing a less than average charity for his colleague from Swanstead.

Walkinshaw was a new M.P. who had won his seat on a platform of an extreme type of Socialism which seemed to Pete and most of his friends to have gone out with the 'thirties. In a violent maiden speech, quite out of tradition with the normal non-controversial contributions which new boys were supposed to make, he had railed against the growing influence of the 'boss class' in the Labour Party and exhorted them to return to the stone tablets of Marxian orthodoxy. This kind of stuff was not new and was readily accepted as not unusual in inexperienced M.P.s. But what had hurt more was his violent attack, in a Sunday paper, on his Labour colleagues who were 'betraying the working class by travelling down to London in First Class sleepers at the expense of the public purse'. And, the next Sunday, they had all been sickened to see a photograph of Walkinshaw stepping self-righteously into his Second Class sleeper compartment, side by side with a photo of five of his colleagues having gins and tonics in the First Class Railbar on the train. The longer service men were firmly convinced that the hours and the hard work which they undertook more than justified the privacy of the First Class sleeper compartment on the London journey, plus a little extra comfort.

Next, had come a savage attack on the 'part-time' M.P.s. 'Just because 40,000 Scottish workers are on part-time work there is no excuse for the people's representatives to work a three-day week in Parliament,' Walkinshaw had screamed to the Press. 'If they are interested in their constituencies, they still have four months' holidays to do this.'

All this had provoked quite a storm and the immediate result had been that the Sunday night train had become much more popular with Scots M.P.s and the Monday night one lost many of its usual passengers.

Things had, by now, settled down a bit and there were only a few M.P.s on the Sunday train but the letters and insults still came in from the public.

'See the latest?' said Pete.

He rummaged in his pocket and produced a grimy piece of paper on which were written some splendid sentiments with a biro pen which had clearly leaked for some time.

'That new bloke is rite,' the message exhorted. 'You politishians is all the same. Promise the earth for our votis, and then Lord-it on the Firste Class with Jins and tonik, and youl get nor more votis from me what abowt the OAPs no Jins for them and your MPs onley do three days works and probible takeing Jins all day, its a ruddey scandil.'

'Who's it from?' asked Gibley with a smile.

'An unknown scribe. But seriously, we must *do* something about that idiot. I've had thirteen letters about it. Should charge up Walkinshaw with the postage. And, whenever I go out, I find everyone looking at me as though I'm plunking from School. My wife, Peggy, had it at the shops all last Tuesday. "Great job your man's got" and "does he do a wee job on the side?" "£65 per week, eh?" and all that,' Pete muttered angrily.

'Can't you bounce him or send him to China or something?' Gibley inquired helpfully.

'And have the papers screaming that we can't stand fair criticism? Not a hope! We'll have to give him a free transfer to the Tories.'

'Get him married off,' said Gibley in another burst of helpfulness. 'That'll cure him.'

'Wouldn't wish him on my worst enemy.'

With this shared dislike having forged a further bond between the two M.P.s, they began the long journey South.

Back in London after a quick taxi ride to dump his suitcase, Gibley made for the Commons and, after picking up his mail (five circulars, three magazines and a dozen letters), he made for the Chief Whip's Office. There was little sign of life but Miss Fordyce, the typist, was there and he gave her a respectful greeting.

'I would like to have a private interview with the Chief Whip. I know how busy he is, but I could manage any time this morning.'

'Is it urgent, Mr. Hobdale?' Miss Fordyce inquired.

'Horn. Gibley Horn. Rossford Constituency' came the instant correction in the hurt voice of someone who thought that his face should really be known by now.

'Of course, Mr Horn, how silly of me. Half awake on Monday morning as usual! I'll certainly speak to the Chief Whip when he comes. Where will you be this morning?'

'Up in the Agency Office until eleven and then in the Library.'

'Right-o. Thank you so much for calling, Mr Horn.'

Gibley trudged away to dictate replies to his twelve constituents feeling a little apprehensive at the prospect of seeing the Chief Whip alone.

✳✳✳   ✳✳✳   ✳✳✳

'Morning, Jones. Good morning, Miss Fordyce.' The Chief Whip stormed into the outer office with a rush and urgency apparently designed to announce that the serious work of the day had begun.

He breezed into his own office through the connecting door, banged his bowler on to the coat-stand, looked hastily round his desk, took a deep breath and then vigorously pressed the buzzer which was fitted beside his telephone.

'Jones!' he shouted through the wall, as if to compensate for any possibility that the buzzer had broken down.

'What's new?' he bawled at the lean and bespectacled figure of his Personal Assistant who crept in silently through the open door.

'The Comms. were at it again at the week-end,' Jones announced, using a highly disrespectful and actionable description of the Left-Wing Tory group, which was causing a little trouble within the Party and had done so ever since the despatch of British troops to restore 'law and order' in the Amerbala Coastal Strip had attracted the criticism of a varied assortment of Afro-Asian nations.

'And what were *THEY* doing? Demonstrating in Trafalgar Square?'

'Much worse. Constable was speaking to a mass rally of wives of university lecturers in Durham.'

'A mass rally?' the Chief Whip queried with disbelief.

'So Constable's Press hand-out said. I'm told that there were nine there including Constable's wife and sister-in-law. But the Press have given it big licks—Page Two in the *Star*, Centre Page lead in the *Commentator* and Front Page side column in the *Mercury*. He said that "informed opinion" in the world was against us and that we should realise that gunboat politics were an unacceptable means of resolving a problem charged with racial tension. Britain, of all countries, should not be engaged in action which could prejudice the effectiveness of the new permanent peace force at UNO.'

'Is that all?'

'It seems to be catching. Colonel Wotherspoon made a speech on pretty orthodox lines, but said that many of his colleagues were concerned about the long-term consequences of acting hastily in the Amerbala problem. Albert Monsley made his usual botch of things on Friday Television, but apparently said that he was sorry that we had sent Dr Iffenzi to the Seychelles.'

'Is it dangerous?'

'The Labour boys might just force a debate next week. Could be some abstentions.'

'Who's in the plot?'

'The usual twenty or so. Long hair, suede shoes, "Let's be nice to the Chinks"—the usual mob, but they might win over some of the new boys.'

'Are they quite solid?'

'As solid as custard pie. Constable has about eight and Harkins ten. Only old Romsey-Wheeler keeps them together. If he would drop out, the Constable and Harkins crowd would be too busy fighting each other to bother about us or these Amerbala scoundrels.'

'And what, my dear Jones, do you suggest we might do to remind Mr Romsey-Wheeler of the error of his ways?'

'Buy him.

'What with?

'A job. Usual stuff. Hint of reshuffle. Shame, if he was passed over because of "entrenched ideological position". Watching him for long time. Very impressed with wide experience. Time ripe for some recognition. Knowledge of foreign affairs could be harnessed to the nation's benefit.'

'Really, Jones, what rubbish! You know that there is no prospect of a reshuffle and that any positions vacated would, in any event, be filled solely on the grounds of ability and experience. And I cannot envisage circumstances, short of revolution, when I might be tempted to recommend Romsey-Wheeler for a post at the F.O. We would be at war in a week!'

'Of course, not the F.O.,' continued Jones and, quite ignoring the implications of the pious statement which he had just heard, he went on—

'If your conscience troubles you, shove him into Agriculture and ditch him quietly at the first farmers' revolt. Romsey-Wheeler would swallow it, and you could forget all about the Comms. for another year.'

'What a squalid concept you have of our happy family here, Jones. I would have thought that the exhilarating experience of working for me over the years would have improved your cynical and jaundiced outlook.'

Jones said nothing but grinned knowingly as though witnessing the devil rebuking sin. And he could not help seeing his boss scribbling down on a pad 'See Martin about Romsey-Wheeler'.

By remaining in the office, after their official chat was thus concluded, Jones indicated that he had further tidings to relate.

'Well, what further disasters have you in store, you horrible man?'

'Gibley Horn wants to see you this morning'

'And who, may I ask, is Gibley Horn?' the Chief asked, using his normal code for indicating that he would be glad to have one of Jones's potted biographies which came in so useful in chats with Members

'Fifty-six years of age, bald, tubby. Elected eleven years ago for Rossford—Scottish County town twenty-five miles from Glasgow. Majority at that time 18,000 which has since steadily declined to 3,000 showing that the electors are acutely aware of his general uselessness. Intensely loyal and never out of step. Has come here only three times in eleven years, each time to swear his undying loyalty to the leadership when there was talk of a *putsch*. Would back King Kong all the way if he was elected to lead the Party.

'Makes few speeches and always bad ones. Last speech four months ago in Roads Debate, when he advocated more roads for Rossford and a new bridge across the Blackross River which his Chamber of Commerce had been moaning about. Last Question in February, to the Minister of Pensions suggesting fuel tokens for Old Age Pensioners to pay for gas and electricity.

'Stays in the Constituency in a big house which he can't afford. Married to Mrs Margaret Horn—daughter of a local builder—plain and pleasant. Son of 24 studying at Yale—physics I think—bright boy called Keith. Daughter married to some boffin in Chester—name Joanna. No grandchildren.

'He has a pretty crummy local organisation. They're beginning to get fed up with Gibley. Slow rumours of the chopper falling before the next election.'

While the Chief could not dispute any of Jones's factual comments, he winced at some of the cynical asides. He had always liked Gibley Horn. Pleasant, courteous, well-behaved, loyal, simple, humble, sincere. Were they talking about the same man?

'If Mr Horn was here, Jones, I would advise him without question to issue a libel writ. I am ashamed of you.'

Again a sly grin appeared on Jones's face as he padded out, saying 'Twelve noon? Coffee for two?'

'Yes. And no poison in the coffee.'

❋❋❋   ❋❋❋   ❋❋❋

As Gibley Horn waited anxiously in the Library with a book propped up before him, he kept a constant lookout for the messenger. At last a tall, austere-looking gentleman, in white tie and tails and with a gold chain round his neck, stopped beside his chair and passed a small note to him.

'The Chief Whip would be glad to see you in his office at 12 noon,' read the message.

After twenty minutes of fidgeting, the Rossford M.P. made his way along the corridor and walked into Miss Fordyce's room, after a hesitant knock.

'I hope I'm not too early,' Gibley mumbled, but a smiling Miss Fordyce lifted the telephone, murmured briefly through it and, as if by magic, the door burst open and out bustled the great man.

'Gibley, dear chap! Come right in. Come in. Come in! Jones, could you manage two coffees right away?'

'I won't keep you a minute, Chief. Know how terribly busy you are,' mumbled the recipient of this rapturous welcome.

'Never too busy for an old friend. I was just saying to Jones that it must be eleven years since you came to this place. How the years speed past!'

Delighted that the Chief Whip should remember his arrival in spite of all the pressures on his time, Gibley nodded agreeably to confirm that, as usual, the Chief was right.

'And how's the family? Is that clever son of yours still lifting the prizes at Yale? Physics he's studying, isn't it?'

'Doing very well, thank you. Had a letter last month.'

'And what about your daughter, Joanna, I think? I'm so bad with names.'

'Yes, getting on splendidly,' Gibley purred, in

delighted astonishment that the Chief should remember so much about him.

'And how is Rossford? Funnily enough, I heard some of our big boys talking about a bridge over the Blackross in your constituency. Apparently you put up a splendid case for it in a speech in the House recently.'

'It's good to know that they listen to my speeches,' Gibley said modestly. 'Some think I don't speak enough.'

'But, of course, they don't, my dear Gibley! They know that you only speak when you have something important to say. Much more effective than these people who are always jumping to their feet with nothing worth saying.

'Why, only a short while ago, I heard some of our members discussing an excellent point which you had raised at Question Time about tokens for gas and electricity for the old folk. I'm afraid the financial position makes it impossible just now, but I know that the Cabinet will want to think seriously about this when things improve. However, I am wasting your time with my blethers. You wanted to speak to me about something?'

Gibley's smiling and satisfied face showed that the time had not been wasted at all. But he quickly got down to the job on hand.

'It's about a political matter, Chief.'

For a minute the Chief looked startled. Surely, Gibley of all people was not getting mixed up with this Amerbala mob. But you never knew what to expect in this game.

'It's my Private Members' Bill.'

The Chief sighed quietly to himself with relief.

'I've been thinking about the possible subjects. And, of course, I have been under pressure from many quarters.'

'And I know that you know enough about this business to separate the cranks from the sensible ones, Gibley. Whatever you pick I know that it will be an excellent cause.'

Gibley warmed to his subject. 'I've been worried for some years about all this chemical stuff the farmers use. Many of my constituents feel that things have gone a bit too far. Food's not what it once was and, I think, that chemical insecticides have a lot to do with it.'

'Of course, to ban insecticides would lose us lots of our farmer friends, Gibley. Hope you're not thinking of that?'

'Certainly not, Chief. But a professor has been in touch with me, indirectly, about some insecticides with a new chemical called BX20. In Paraguay, where it has been used for some years, there have been out-breaks of all kinds of diseases. It could be dangerous, it seems. My legal advisers say that it would be difficult to ban BX20 but, apparently, it wipes out some harmless insect called the Spotted Hummerfly and, if we protected this in a Private Bill, we could effectively stop BX20 being used in this country.'

The Chief thought quickly. There might, possibly, be something in it but, if there was, the newspapers or some of the livelier M.P.s would have pounced on it. If it was entirely cranky nonsense, however, the Bill would be slaughtered and no great harm done, so long as the Party was not tied to it. He could always arrange for another Tory to move its rejection if the Bill caused any adverse comment in farming circles.

'Well, I can't claim to be an expert on BX20, Gibley, but I have enough confidence in you to know that you will have thought it all out carefully.'

'Do you think the Party will support me?' asked Gibley.

'On a Private Bill?' queried the Chief Whip. 'It would be quite wrong for us to give guidance on a Private Bill, Gibley. We never do. Other than in the most exceptional circumstances,' he added hastily, thinking of Cranshaw's Penal Reform Bill the previous year.

'If we did, it would mean that the other side would move against it and the best Bills are those which can get support from all Parties. However, I'm quite sure that when our boys see that you are promoting this, many will want to support it. I have no objection whatsoever to your bringing in such a Bill and I know that Central Office will be delighted to help with the drafting side of things.'

'Well, actually, I've seen to that myself.' Gibley produced the draft which Miss Phillimore had given him and pushed it, proudly, across the desk.

The Chief glanced at the Bill. He hurriedly flipped through the pages and put on an air of being impressed.

'It looks splendid, old boy. Excellent! Splendid! Well,' he continued, rising slowly in his seat, 'I'm afraid that I shall have to go; I have to see Sir Oliver at twelve-thirty. I'll certainly mention your Bill to him. I know he will be *very* interested.'

'Thank you so much for your advice, Chief,' Gibley sounded apologetic. 'It's been a great help.'

'Not at all, Gibley. Glad to see you at any time and I really think that with our long friendship we might drop the "Chief". I should be delighted if we could just make it "Bernard",' he suggested pleasantly.

'Thank you very much,' Gibley hesitated, '. . . Bernard,' and then made his way out after a firm handshake.

What an excellent chap the Chief was, Gibley thought as he walked through the Lobby. And fancy him remembering the speech! If they got that bridge over the Blackross what a feather in his cap it would be. He wondered who the 'big boys' had been, who were talking about this. The Chancellor? The Secretary of State? The Transport Minister? Or perhaps all three? He must try to make another speech about it soon. Strike while the iron was hot.

And now, where had he left his brief-case? Always losing it in this place. . . .

Back in the Whip's Office, the Chief sat quietly in his seat for a while. What a pleasant chap Gibley was! So respectful! So appreciative! What a change from the normal ones who came into his office with their arrogant threats and blusterings. He must remember the old chap when they next talked about the Honours List. If anyone deserved a mention, it was old Gibley. How on earth had he got mixed up in this game?

As he strode out of his room Jones, ever anxious to

keep up to date, inquired waspishly, 'What did the old fool want?'

For once, unimpressed by Jones's cynical patter, the Chief looked angrily at his assistant:

'He asked for permission to raise a force of volunteers to stop the British colonial imperialist troops from attacking the peace-loving peoples of the Amerbala Coastal Strip,' he spat out, 'and I agreed, of course.'

'Did he leave an address in Amerbala where I can send on the staff Christmas benefit appeal?' came the sarcastic rejoinder; but on seeing the fierce look in the Chief's eye, Jones decided that the time was not opportune for more lighthearted pleasantry and he immersed himself studiously in some papers.

'Something biting the Chief?' asked Miss Fordyce anxiously.

'A Spotted Hummerfly, no doubt,' replied Jones, looking inquisitively at some notes scribbled on the Chief's blotting-pad.

✳✳✳   ✳✳✳   ✳✳✳

Having spoken to the Chief Whip and having had a delightful reception, Gibley now addressed himself to the task of finding supporters to sponsor his Bill which would have to be submitted the following week.

John Knox-Crichton had been mentioned by Miss Phillimore. Fancy, him being involved with the Insect Friendship League! Wonder where he is? Gibley looked at his watch. Almost 1 p.m. Should see him in the

Members' Dining Room. So he strode along the corridor, stopping for a brief glance at the latest news on the tapes. 'American Moonshot expected in January.' Hm. Believe *that* when it comes. Unreliable things these rockets. 'Go Ahead for Monorail Project.' And not before time. The roads were getting more and more cluttered up. 150 m.p.h.? Two and a half hours to Glasgow? That would make old B.R. sit up. 'Food riots in Bengal.' Nothing new in that. Always thought they gave them independence too soon. Gibley's natural friendly attitude to the Indians had suffered a rude shock when, in a conversation with the Labour Agent after the Rossford count, he had found out that his Party had also been promised the block vote of the Rossford Indian population. And so had the Liberals and Scottish Nationalists! Wonder what they really did? Probably tried to use the ballot papers as bus tickets. 'Electricity Supply Dispute still unresolved.' That Bill allowing the Government to ban strikes for forty days had really been a washout. There were just as many strikes as before and simply forty days more to organise and finance them. What could be done about these strikes? Might serve the leaders right to send them to the Seychelles with Dr Iffenzi. Nothing much else in the news.

He wandered into the Members' Dining Room which was quiet, as was usual on a Monday. He looked at the Tory tables to see if he could spot Knox-Crichton. Eventually he sighted him up at a table near the window engrossed in talk with Iain Constable and his friend, Walter Hughes. Trying to get John involved in one of these Left-Wing exercises no doubt, Gibley thought. But they're wasting their time with Knox-Crichton.

As he made for the table, Knox-Crichton welcomed him effusively: 'Come and sit down, Gibley. Delighted to see you looking so well!'

The more than usually warm welcome confirmed Gibley's suspicions that the other two had been trying to badger him to join some plot or other. Messrs Constable and Hughes addressed themselves vigorously to the celery soup, knowing that any talk of revolt or even of criticism of the official policy was impossible in Gibley Horn's presence.

It was a funny place, the Members' Dining Room. There was strict segregation between the Labour and Tory ends of the room, Members talked freely amongst themselves and any worthwhile news or gossip could usually be picked up over lunch or dinner.

'And where do the Liberals sit?' an inquisitive lady had asked him after he had spoken on Parliamentary customs to the Rossford Townswomen's Guild. 'On the fence, as usual,' he had replied, amidst uproarious laughter. But there they were, right in the middle of the room with their own special table. And how delighted they had been when an extra leaf had been needed to be added after the last election. And poor old Donald Anderson, the sole Scottish Nationalist, had been so confused at the rigid rules that, rather than sit with the Tories, the Socialists or the Liberals, he had sentenced himself to five years of steak pie, cod and bridies, all with chips, in the 'easy-eats' buffet downstairs.

Now that Gibley had arrived at the table, the conversation became general, but he noted with delight that Constable and Hughes were more advanced in their meals than John Knox-Crichton and he would, therefore, have a chance to speak to the latter privately.

At last the rebels departed and he got down to it.

'John, old man, you'll know that I was lucky in the Private Bill draw?'

'Yes, I did hear that,' John replied without enthusiasm. For the past few years Knox-Crichton had carefully avoided putting his own name in for the ballot. Private Bills were a nuisance. All that happened was that you got loads of cranks writing to you and it would mean staying on for a Friday—all right viewed from a distance, but tiresome when the day approached. Few of these Bills ever became law so it tended to be a waste of time.

'I've been looking at many possibilities,' Gibley continued, 'and one of them was put to me by some people from the Insect Friendship League.'

'Not that crowd!' John interrupted with a groan, 'they're nuts, scatty. Should be banned!'

'But I understood that you were one of their supporters. Gave money and all that.'

'Of course I do. I'm mad also, you see. Seriously, I have a very old aunt who has a thing about the Insect League. She's given them most of her money. My wife insists that I should humour her and so I send them a tenner at Christmas and ask a question about insecticides every six months or so. If you're daft enough to bring in one of their Bills, I'll be forced to support it, or life will be Hell at home.'

Rather distressed at his friend's response, but desperately anxious to find out how serious he was, Gibley proceeded to tell the whole story about why he had taken an interest in the Spotted Hummerfly. When he came to the bit about the BX20 preparations being used extensively in Paraguay but not in America, where the stuff was produced, Knox-Crichton came alive.

'Say that again.'

The story was repeated.

'There might be something big here, old boy. Dynamite if it's true. Better do some checking up.'

'Who should I check with?'

'Shove down some questions. It's cheaper than phoning the Embassy.'

'But, seriously, will you support the Bill if I bring it in?'

'I'll have to, for Aunt Emily's sake. But I think you're nuts.'

'Splendid,' said Gibley. 'But what about these questions, what should I ask?'

'Question One—What quantity of the chemical known as BX20 has been imported from the U.S.A. in each of the past five years and what was the cost in each year?' Knox-Crichton scribbled down the question on the menu as he spoke. 'That one should be asked to the Board of Trade.

'Question Two—for the Minister of Agriculture. What information has he regarding the extent to which chemical insecticides containing BX20 are used in Britain and in foreign countries, and what specific information he has regarding the position in the United States and Paraguay. These should nail down the facts. They must give you answers. If there's anything to hide it will show through.'

'Thank you very much indeed, John, I'll put these in right away.' Gibley put the menu with the questions in his pocket.

'I saw you pinching that menu,' came a cry from the next table and, looking round, Gibley saw the happy rotund face and figure of Sir Andrew Mellin, a popular if somewhat eccentric member of the Party. Sensing that this was a good day for him Gibley decided to test his luck.

'Just taking this home to show the wife how well fed I am here. By the way, Andrew, like to sponsor my Private Bill?'

'If it's anything to do with illegitimate children or bingo, the answer is No. My constituents are against sin. At least they expect their M.P. to be against it.' Mellin's fat, Falstaffian face quivered with laughter as he spoke.

'No. Nothing like that.'

'What's it called then, old boy. Spill!'

'The Spotted Hummerfly Protection Bill.'

'And what the blazes does that do?' asked Sir Andrew in astonishment.

'Protects Spotted Hummerflies,' interrupted John Knox-Crichton. 'I've signed for it—they're splendid creatures, these Hummerflies—need protecting. What about it, Andrew?'

'Get lost,' said Sir Andrew. 'What's happened to you, Gibley, gone all health food and early swims?'

'Don't laugh too soon, Andrew boy,' John Knox-Crichton chipped in again, 'I think Gibley is on to something pretty big.'

The dining-room was emptying as 2.30 p.m. approached. It was the time for Questions in the House and the Minister of Health was at the Dispatch Box. The three M.P.s made their way to the Chamber.

After listening to the first ten or so questions which appeared to be essentially parish pump matters of no general interest, like 'Will the Minister take all possible steps to speed up the building of the new hospital at Wonburgh?' 'Will the Minister take steps to improve the casualty service at Abutermarry?' 'Will the Minister endeavour to improve facilities for young doctors?' . . .

The answer was always 'Yes' but, no doubt, the Questions would come up again in seven weeks, when the Minister was on duty at the Dispatch Box again.

Gibley wandered out of the Chamber and went along to the Table Office to put in the questions, which he carefully copied out from the menu. For an oral answer he would have to wait for weeks but, it was simply information he wanted, so a written reply would do. He dated the questions for Friday and handed them in to the Clerk who, after a quick glance, agreed to accept them.

Having put in the questions, he wandered round the corridors awhile hoping to see Mr Bothwell, the Labour M.P. for Darnley South, and Mr Forbes, the 'nice' new Liberal, both of whom were expected by Miss Phillimore to support the Bill.

In the process he came across old Will Francis who,

at eighty-one years of age, was only too glad to sign anything for anyone who would stop for a chat and listen to some of his reminiscences.

'Spotted whats?' he asked, without really being interested in the reply. Then he went on to tell Gibley about what Ramsay MacDonald had said to him and, more important, what he had said to Ramsay MacDonald and how this had changed the whole course of history. After listening for fifteen minutes, Gibley felt that he had paid the price for the signature and he moved on.

David Forbes lived up to his reputation of being a 'nice' Liberal by signing the Bill, although he did not appear to have any strong recollection of writing to the Insect Friendship League.

'So many circulars at Election time,' he explained. 'No harm in sending agreeable replies, although I don't think that I was specific to any of them.'

Jonathan Bothwell had, however, been less co-operative and had flatly denied having committed himself or sold his soul in any way to the League. However, Will Francis's signature would do instead and would give the Bill the semblance of being 'All-Party'.

Having got over the obvious hurdles, Gibley Horn decided to put through a call to the League to say that he had burned his boats and that the Insect League could look forward to the future with hope, if not confidence, that their cause would be pressed in the House of Commons.

'A cordial greeting to you and all friends of dumb animals and insects', had been the reply at the other end of the line before he could even introduce himself and get through to Miss Phillimore. This had rather taken him aback as he shrank instinctively from having any dealings with strange people. However, the joy and delight of Miss Phillimore more than compensated for this and he arranged to meet the Executive of the League in the House the following Monday at tea-time to discuss 'tactics' and, Gibley hoped, to get material for his speech.

The rest of the week went quietly enough. Having settled on his Bill, Gibley decided to make a speech on Thursday, when a Road Safety measure was being debated. He collected facts and figures from the Library and from old Hansards. Then he prepared some punch lines about how good roads and bridges could help to prevent accidents.

'If I could take an example from my own Constituency where, for years, I have been advocating the construction of a new bridge over the Blackross River with the active support and co-operation of my local Chamber of Commerce . . .' he found himself thinking aloud.

But when Thursday came, forty Members or more were trying to speak and, by the time 8.30 p.m. came along, although Gibley jumped up vigorously every time someone sat down, in the hope of catching the Speaker's eye, it was clear that his splendid speech was not going to be delivered. All he could do was to file it away in his locker and hope that some other subjects would be discussed soon when he might be more successful.

The system in the Commons could be exasperating, he reflected. After the opening Front Bench speakers had finished, usually around 4.30 or 5 p.m., those M.P.s wishing to speak jumped up like Jack-in-the-Boxes in their places. There might be as many as fifty. The Speaker would call one and the others would sit patiently listening. When this speech was finished, the forty-nine would bob up and another would be called. As only about ten speakers could be lucky in a normal debate, this meant a lot of disappointed men whose speeches were not delivered. You could never tell who was going to be called. You couldn't 'fix' it with anyone. The Speaker, although chosen from the membership of the House, was entirely independent and chose whomsoever he thought should speak for that day. You had a better chance if you were an 'expert' on the subject, or if you had been unsuccessful in being called in other debates in the recent past.

But clearly the Speaker did not consider that Gibley Horn fell into either of these categories so far as the Road Safety Bill was concerned.

As he had been deprived of the opportunity of speaking, Gibley decided to boycott the 'wind up' speeches beginning at 9 p.m. The Opposition had moved an amendment, so there was to be a vote at 10. He filled up his time by having a coffee and sandwiches in the cafeteria and chatting about nothing in particular with Scottish colleagues who were also filling in time till the vote.

'All those in favour say Aye,' cried the Speaker as ten o'clock struck. And there was a loud roar from the

Opposition Members anxious to show approval, first for their amendment, but more for the splendidly aggressive speech from their Front Bench speaker.

'Those against say No.' A mild ripple of 'Noes' echoed across the Government Benches whose members were still smarting under the forceful attack from the Opposition.

'I think the Noes have it,' said the Speaker with a smile.

'Aye' came a chorus from the Opposition.

'Division!' cried the Speaker and his call was taken up by the attendants outside the Chamber while bells began to ring throughout the building, much to the consternation of the visitors assembled in the Central Lobby.

The bells were designed, not to call the faithful to prayer, but to the Division Lobbies. There was one Lobby on each side of the Chamber entrance, with Whips posted at each entrance to ensure that Members went into the right Lobby irrespective of whether they understood the intricacies of Parliamentary procedure and, indeed, whether or not they were aware of the subject under discussion.

Having tramped faithfully through the 'Noes' Lobby Gibley did not bother to wait in the House for the result to be declared. With a majority of sixty for the Government in the House, there was little excitement these days in the votes except where abstentions were likely.

The amendment having been defeated, the Bill was given an unopposed Second Reading and the word spread round that, except for those who had a special interest in the fishing industry on the North East Coast, which was the subject of the Adjournment Debate, there was nothing to stop the Members drifting off.

And Gibley did drift off, thankfully, to the Tube station and from there to Euston and the night train back to Glasgow.

✻✻✻   ✻✻✻   ✻✻✻

Travelling back home, Gibley thought out his coming week-end activities. Friday was free, thank God; but Saturday would be a bad day. In the morning he had one of his 'surgeries' in the Conservative Rooms; in the afternoon he had to open a Bazaar and in the evening he had to entertain the Chairman of the Association and his wife to dinner at home. But at least Friday was free. Margaret and he usually made as quickly as possible for the coast where they could have a leisurely walk round one of the municipal golf courses and a quiet lunch at McLellan's Tea Room, where he could usually count on not being recognised.

The important thing was to get away before the phone started ringing. Many a Friday had been spoiled completely by his hanging around too long.

It was about a quarter to eight in the morning when he drove up the driveway to his home. He knew that Margaret would have everything ready for a quick getaway. But, as he stopped at the front door, he saw Margaret was standing there looking agitated.

'Quick, Gibley. Central Office on the phone. They say it's urgent!'

Gibley hated hurrying at any time, particularly when he arrived home for his week-end's relaxation. But nevertheless he dashed to the telephone.

'Caledonian T.V., Big Ben Probe Programme tonight. We've been let down at the last minute. Can you fill in? Studios at 6 p.m.,' explained the anxious voice from Edinburgh.

'What short notice!' Gibley reacted angrily. 'I have a *very* full programme of constituency engagements today.'

After a further short exchange in which he made it more than ever clear that it would be immensely inconvenient, Gibley agreed with apparent reluctance to 'do' the show. It was a bore but, all the same, he couldn't afford to let these television opportunities slip by. Gibley felt that, in any event, he did not get his fair share of them. Some of his colleagues always seemed to be on the air, while he hadn't had a shot for about a year. Everyone seemed to watch these days, and a T.V. programme had more effect than making ten speeches in the House.

'What's the programme about and who am I on with?' he asked.

'Electricity, hydro-electric stations, atomic power, consumer prices, the lot', came the answer. 'The Party has quite a record there. Hope you'll make the most of it. It's in the pamphlets, but you'll remember the Debate last month when the Minister went over it all. And you're on with Davie Mason for Labour and Bill Grierson for the Libs. O.K.?'

Davie Mason? Oh dear! He was one of the aggressive Labour types. This wasn't so good. He would have to read up the stuff.

'Fine,' Gibley replied cheerfully. 'I'll make short work of that lot, but I've left the pamphlet in London: could you get the Glasgow Office to send one down out here? I will probably be out in the Constituency, so tell them to put it through the letter-box.'

If they got back from the coast by 3.30, Gibley calculated, that would give him plenty of time to mug up the stuff and get to the studios in time.

'I'm on television again tonight, Margaret,' Gibley advised his wife as he put the receiver down, just as if it was a regular occurrence, 'so we'd better get moving right away.'

Immediately the telephone rang again vigorously.

'Bother!' said his wife. 'Do you think we should answer it?'

'It'll be Central Office again about the television show. Nobody else would phone at this time on a Friday.'

But it was not Edinburgh. It was London.

'Mr Horn? Mr Gibley Horn,' came the anxious inquiry. 'Jamieson here. Whip's Office. I'm speaking from my home. We tried to catch you before you left the House last night. You will have seen in the Press that Rossford Chemicals are closing their factory at Manendon? Archie Dundas, your Labour member for Rossfordshire East, has a Private Notice Question down for answer at eleven o'clock today. You're the only Tory in the County and the Chief Whip thinks you should be here for it. Can you come down right away?'

Why had he bothered to answer the blasted phone? Gibley stamped his foot.

'Couldn't possibly make it, old boy. That's in three hours' time,' he declared with attempted nonchalance.

'We've looked up, sir,' said the Whip's Assistant. 'If you get a taxi to the Airport at your end for the nine o'clock plane down, another taxi at this end should get you to the House just before eleven. I think you should try. The Chief is very worried. Most of our Scots Members are away home and you are directly involved in this one.'

'But I'm on television tonight!'

'You have plenty of time to get back, sir, the two-thirty plane to Glasgow would do.'

Illusions of a quiet week-end shattered, poor old Gibley, without even taking off his coat and without taking his case from the car, hurriedly told Margaret the sad news, got into his car again and sped towards the Airport.

It would be a tight job to get to the Airport in time for the plane, but he might make it before the morning rush. It was now 7.55 a.m. precisely and, if he made the Airport by 8.45, he should squeeze on. Just as well that he had a spare air warrant in his wallet.

But he hated flying. He hated rushing. He hated the whole miserable business. Why did he bother? But if he gave up Parliament, what about money? What in earth could he do at his age?

And there were these blasted pains in his chest again! He hadn't had any for a month, but there was that feeling again like a tight iron bar.

He drove into the Airport car park at 8.39 a.m. precisely after a hectic journey during which he had broken most of the Highway Code, sped on foot towards the Airport buildings and rushed to the ticket desk.

'Yes, if you hurry, Mr Horn. Sorry, First Class is full, but we can get you on Tourist.'

Blast! That meant these cramped seats which were more appropriate to a cattle boat. And no newspapers to read. But it would have to do.

As he climbed up the gangway to the aircraft, he felt distinctly ill. He still gripped his heavy case, not having had time to check it in at the Airport.

In minutes, after he had pushed his way through the packed body of passengers to one of the few vacant seats, bumping not a few of them with his case, the plane's engines roared and it sped along the runway.

This was the bit he always hated. It was tolerable when you had room to move and look around in the First Class but, where he was, he felt completely stifled with two grim-faced and portly matrons between him and the small window at the side of the plane. And to think that he should have been happily on his way to the golf course by now. It was heartbreaking!

'Excuse me,' said one of the ladies at his side. 'Are you not Mr Horn, our M.P. in Rossford? Shouldn't you be down at the House of Commons?'

My God! It was going to be one of those journeys!

'I was there at ten p.m. last night, but I had to come up to the Constituency for an important meeting early this morning. And now I have to be back in the House for eleven this morning.'

'Don't you start work till eleven in the morning? No wonder the country's in a state!'

'Only on a Friday. Other days it's two-thirty p.m., Mrs—mm——'

'Miss McQuarrie. Miss Molly McQuarrie,' came the instant correction. 'And this is my sister Sarah.'

'Well, although we start officially at two-thirty p.m., there is lots to do before then. We have Committees in the morning. We have to answer correspondence. We have to prepare speeches.'

'And do you make many speeches, Mr Horn?' inquired Miss Sarah looking as though she knew the answer.

'I try to speak only when I have something important to say,' Gibley replied a little huffily. 'Actually, I tried to make a speech last night, but the Speaker didn't call me.'

'Why's that?' Miss Molly asked suspiciously. 'Haven't you been behaving yourself?'

'That's nothing to do with it, Miss McQuarrie. You see lots of M.P.s want to speak each day and we only get a chance once every few months.'

'Really, Mr Horn!' chipped in Miss Sarah, by now clearly convinced that she was being told the tall story of the year, 'that new Labour Member, Mr Walkinshaw, seems to make speeches almost every day. How does he manage it?'

'Well, he doesn't actually make many speeches'— Gibley was now looking a trifle flustered— 'most of the stories in the Press are when he interjects in Question Time or talks to the reporters. He's always speaking to journalists or issuing statements. Not speaking in the House at all.'

'Well the papers always talk about his speeches in Parliament. And couldn't you interject at Question Time too?' Miss Sarah assumed a rather bullying tone.

'You must do a lot of travelling, Mr Horn,' Miss Molly interrupted. 'Do you have to pay your own fares?'

'Not when we are travelling on Parliamentary business to and from the Constituency,' Gibley answered, feeling by now completely trapped in this airborne cage.

'And I suppose that this *is* Parliamentary business?' Miss Sarah inquired, looking with barely concealed disgust at Mr Horn as though he was pinching the Parish Church Funds.

'Certainly. I'm travelling to Parliament from the Constituency.'

And so the conversation proceeded as the plane lurched and shook, much to the consternation of the Rossford M.P. and his stomach.

When the coffee came along, Gibley's hand was shaking so much that he spilled a fair measure of it over Miss Molly's coat. The physical contortions, which he was required to perform in order to wipe up the mess as best he could and at the same time to pacify Miss Molly, took such a while that he had no time to ask for more coffee.

In a final gesture of peace-making, he took out a packet of 'House of Commons' cigarettes and offered the ladies one of these unique and interesting objects.

'No thank you. We don't smoke,' came the reply, but the ladies were clearly interested in the splendid-looking package which had the gold crest of the Commons on the front.

'And do you get these free too?'

'No, we don't!' Gibley answered angrily. 'They cost more than the normal kind.'

'Of course, you get a very large salary, don't you? Sixty-five pounds a week?' Miss Sarah advised triumphantly.

Sensing that it was pointless trying to justify himself before the ladies and thoroughly convinced that he had by now lost their votes, Gibley decided that it was the appropriate time to comment on the weather, and with other small talk the journey proceeded until the plane touched down at Heathrow at 10 a.m. precisely.

❀❀❀   ❀❀❀   ❀❀❀

By the time he reached the Airport building it was 10.10 and Gibley hailed one of the cabs which were parked outside.

'House of Commons, Members' Entrance. I'm in a hurry,' he blurted out.

'Cost you four pounds, guv.'

'Very well,' said Gibley, boiling internally at this daylight robbery but not having the energy to protest openly.

'Pretty exciting times you're having,' said the taxi-man chattily as he put his foot on the accelerator.

'Yes, we are,' said Gibley, 'but I've had a most

tiring morning and don't feel like having a discussion on the political situation.' He was sorry to be so brusque, but he had spent many an agonising taxi journey having to lean forward to hear the spasmodic comments which taximen shouted through the connecting window, and his only desire was to lie back in the cab and relax. After all, he was paying four pounds for it.

'You a Tory?' came the next inquiry.

'As a matter of fact I am.'

'Hm,' came the non-committal reply from the taximan. He had always known they were an arrogant crowd of Bs. Well here was one who was going to have a bumpy journey. . . .

The traffic was very heavy and Gibley was frequently alarmed by sudden starts and stops.

'I want to get there alive,' he shouted through the window.

'Thought you were in a hurry,' replied the taximan, smiling to himself at this authoritative proof that his efforts were being rewarded with success.

By the time they drove through the New Palace Yard gates at five to eleven Gibley felt wretched. Dumping his case at the Members' Entrance, he sped up the stairs towards the Chamber. As he approached the door of the Members' Lobby he saw that the Speaker's Procession was approaching and he would have no chance of getting in before it. So he would have to wait until after Prayers and get in quickly before the Question was asked.

'Speaker!' announced the attendant in a powerful

military shout to the handful of Members sitting in the House to warn them that the Procession was approaching and that they would soon have to rouse themselves and stand up when both Speaker and Chaplain entered.

As the procession strode majestically into the Chamber the doors were closed and soon could be heard the distant sound of the prayer which had traditionally been made for decades, 'God be merciful unto us. . . .'

And its repetition would give the Rossford M.P. about four minutes to collect his thoughts.

Rossford Chemicals? That was the big building with the unusually shaped chimneys just off the Glasgow Road. Several hundred workers in his Constituency were employed there and he remembered meeting some chap at a cocktail party who had introduced himself as the manager. It would be bad if the factory closed, and involved quite a bit of unemployment, on top of the recent closure of the last coal-mine in the area last year.

But what question could he ask? What steps will the Minister take to provide other employment? Is the Minister aware that this news will be greeted with alarm in Rossfordshire? Is the Minister aware that the unemployment rate in the county is already 4 per cent?

Any of these would do, Gibley thought. If Archie Dundas picked on any one of these for his own supplementary question he could ask one of the two others. He scribbled down the alternatives on an order paper which he had grabbed from the window of the Vote Office in the Members' Lobby.

'And now may the grace of God . . .'

The doors swung open and Gibley stepped smartly through and bustled along to his normal seat in the middle of the third bench below the gangway, on the Speaker's right-hand side.

He had a quick look round. There on the Government Front Bench in front of him to the left was Ian Forbes-Paton, the Minister of State at the Board of Trade who had clearly been brought in, in the absence of the President of the Board of Trade, to answer Archie's question. And there on the opposite benches was Archie Dundas himself, tight-lipped, glowering at Gibley Horn and looking somewhat surprised to see him. No doubt he had been ready to remark on 'the absence of the County's only Tory in this alarming emergency'. Just as well that he had come down.

Mind you, it was surprising that the Speaker had accepted the Private Notice Question, particularly on a Friday. But there were more of those Friday morning questions ever since the Select Committee had recommended making Friday more of a 'working day' in the House and not just an opportunity for the faithful few to argue about abstract non-controversial motions and Bills, while the majority were home or at their Constituencies.

The Speaker rose to his feet and announced in slow measured terms: 'Mr Dundas, Private Notice Question.'

'Mr Speaker, I wish to ask the President of the Board of Trade a question of which I have given him Private Notice—if he will make a statement on the announcement made yesterday by the Board of Rossford Chemicals that they intend to close, immediately, their factory at Manendon in Rossfordshire which employs seven hundred people.'

This was Archie at his best. Spitting out the words and glowering at the Minister as though he was personally, rather than only fictionally, responsible for the closure of the factory and the unemployment and hardship which would result in 700 Scottish homes.

The Minister rose and put some papers on the Dispatch Box and prepared to read his answer from the statement, prepared by his Civil Servants. Poor chap, thought Gibley, probably never heard of Rossford Chemicals before last night.

'I am advised,' the Minister began confidently, without a quaver in his voice, 'that the Board of Rossford Chemicals announced yesterday that they will be forced to close their chemical factory at Manendon because of the combined effects of heavy losses incurred by the factory in recent years and a reduction in the demand for the particular chemicals produced at Manendon. My Right Honourable Friend, the President of the Board of Trade, regrets this, but believes that the firm had no alternative in view of the competitive position in the chemical industry and the strain which further losses would put on the financial position of the company. The Ministry of Labour, through its local offices, will take every possible step to find suitable alternative work for the men and women made redundant in consequence of the closure.'

The Minister sat down knowing full well that this answer would fail to satisfy his questioner who was sitting on the edge of his seat ready to pounce.

Archie Dundas jumped to his feet.

And at the same time Gibley Horn on the Government side and about five of Archie's Scottish Labour colleagues rose from their seats to let the Speaker know that they would like to enter the argument also.

'Is the Minister aware that this news will be greeted with alarm in Rossfordshire? How will the seven hundred men and women be found other jobs when there is already an unemployment rate of four per cent? And has the Government any specific plans to provide other employment, or can they only offer pious hopes?'

Archie sat down triumphantly and glanced up expectantly at the Press Gallery where the Scottish newspaper reporters could be seen scribbling furiously.

Gibley was in a panic. Every one of his supplementary questions asked already. What the blazes could he ask? And when the Minister had finished his reply to Archie he would have to ask something new. He was no good at this impromptu stuff.

But the Minister was already on his feet:

'I appreciate the Honourable Member for Rossfordshire East's concern in this matter, and can assure him that the Government would have been glad if the closure could have been avoided but to keep the Manendon factory open would have placed the firm's other works at London and Manchester in jeopardy. I am well aware of the unemployment rate in Rossfordshire ('You'll hear more about it,' interjected Willie McClelland from the Labour benches) and my Ministry will give every possible assistance to firms seeking to establish new factories in the district.'

He sat down.

'Mr Horn,' called the Speaker, and Gibley rose to his feet, looking flustered and confused.

'Maiden speech!' Archie Dundas shouted across the Chamber amid some laughter, this being the traditional and cruel way of drawing attention to the fact that a Member did not participate a great deal in the activities of the House.

'While accepting the Minister's statement that the factory had to close . . .' Gibley began hesitantly.

('What do your constituents think?' interjected another Labour Member. 'He hasn't seen them for years,' came the helpful reply from another.)

This riled Gibley who had intended to add to his opening question the words 'to avoid more jobs being lost in other areas of the country'. But the staccato insults from the other side had put these out of his mind.

'I live in my constituency and know their views a lot better than you do,' Gibley retorted angrily at the anonymous critics.

Instantly the Speaker was on his feet.

'The Honourable Member has been here long enough to know that he must not accuse me of not knowing something.'

Damn! He had been caught out in that old procedural point which was the traditional Parliamentary 'Off Side' trap. An M.P. always has to speak through the Chair and say that 'The Hon. Member opposite doesn't know . . .' or 'the Hon. Member for X does not know'. Otherwise, the word 'You' reflected on the Speaker.

'I'm sorry, Mr Speaker,' Gibley blurted out, 'but I'm fed up at being constantly interrupted by these hooligans on the benches opposite.'

By now, looking severe, the Speaker rose to interrupt him and said sharply, 'Hooligan is not a Parliamentary manner of referring to Hon. Members. I must ask the Honourable Member for Rossford to withdraw that expression.

'My apologies,' said Gibley, now thoroughly flustered. 'I withdraw that comment.'

Turning to the Minister he continued, 'About this factory closure, I would like to ask the Minister . . .

Instantly, the Speaker was on his feet again.

'Parliamentary time is short and the Hon. Member for Rossford has taken up quite some time with these points of Order. I think the Minister should reply to the points which he has made and we can then press on.'

Gibley sat down with a look of hopeless despondency on his face and the Minister rose to reply in obvious embarrassment. He had no points to answer from the sole questioner from the Tory side.

'I am well aware,' he said, 'of my Hon. Friend's deep interest in the welfare of his constituents.' This was always a safe start to any reply to a colleague in the same Party, but its effect was rather lost when Archie Dundas shouted out, 'He wants them all on the dole,' receiving a glance of disapproval in so doing from the Speaker who was anxious to show his impartiality after having slapped Gibley Horn down. The Minister continued, ignoring the interruption.

'But it is a most responsible attitude to recognise that it is the wider interest of the nation which we are here in Parliament to safeguard and not just narrow parochial interests.'

Gibley jumped to his feet again in consternation. Surely the Minister hadn't seriously thought that any M.P. would welcome the closure of one of the main factories in his constituency. But he had had his chance and the Speaker next called James McKinnon, one of the shrewdest and most experienced Scottish Members on the Opposition benches.

'Would the Minister realise that, unlike the Member for Rossford, Scottish Members do not welcome the closure of this great chemical factory and will he not agree that, if the Government had not repealed the Redundancy Payments Bill which, under the previous Government, provided very real assistance to displaced workers, the hardship and misery stemming from this closure could have been greatly reduced?'

If the Minister had been quicker in the uptake, he would have realised the need to deny the accusation about the Rossford M.P. at the beginning of the question, but being new and enthusiastic, he jumped at the reference to the Redundancy Payments Bill and forgot about poor old Gibley.

'The Hon. Member must be aware that the Redundancy Payments Bill, introduced as a cheap electioneering gimmick by the Party opposite, effectively sabotaged the mobility of labour which is essential in a dynamic economy. As regards the responsibility of Her Majesty's Government, he must likewise be aware that, faced with the catastrophic economic legacy, which they inherited after the Hon. Gentlemen opposite scuttled from office, unpopular decisions were necessary. The electors of Rossford must realise this as well as the electorate of the nation.' This spirited response produced some cheers from the handful of Government supporters on the benches.

But Gibley Horn was not one of the enthusiasts. He bounced up again, anxious to retrieve his reputation and correct the misinterpretation of his opinions.

'Mr Speaker,' he began.

'I do not wish to remind the Member for Rossford again that many Hon. Members are anxious to question the Minister and he has already had his opportunity. I must ask him to resume his seat,' declared the Speaker.

'Mr Anderson,' he called, inviting the sole Scottish Nationalist Member to speak.

Donald Anderson, tall, burly, with a fanatical intensity strangely out of place in relation to his formidable figure, weighed in with his favourite question.

'Is this not yet one further example of the Government's cynical disregard for Scotland and their neglect of the nation at the expense of the prosperous areas of the South?'

This question produced sarcastic cheers from both sides of the House who still found Donald very much of a novelty.

'No, Sir,' replied the Minister with a good-natured smile.

The buzz of murmurs during the last few exchanges

made it clear that most of those present believed that they had heard quite enough about Rossford Chemicals and its 700 workers. The Speaker rose once again to declare: 'We must press on with the business. The Clerk will now read the Orders of the Day.'

The Clerk, looking strangely naked without his wig, which had recently been removed after a Select Committee Report had suggested the abolition of all uncomfortable uniforms and headgear, stood up and read in a high-pitched but authoritative tone.

'Land Tenure Amendment Bill. Second Reading.'

At this, those M.P.s present, who had a special interest in land tenure, looked more interested and started casting shifty glances round the benches to make an estimate of the numbers of their colleagues who would be seeking to speak on the Bill. Fortunately there were not many on the benches, and most of those wishing to speak would probably be called. So, attending the House on a Friday was well worth while!

The Solicitor General rose to introduce the Bill.

'The purpose of this Bill, which is essentially non-controversial, is to repeal Section 148. . . .'

Gibley Horn was not, of course, the slightest bit interested in the Land Tenure Bill, which probably only applied to England and Wales. But he was aware of the excited whispering and joking going on amongst the Scottish Labour Members on the opposite benches. As they kept looking in his direction, Gibley knew that they were enjoying some jest at his expense.

What a dirty crowd they were! They couldn't care less about the Rossford Chemicals factory or about the men who would be put out of work. All that they were interested in was scoring a political point which would put one of their opponents in a bad light. And, what annoyed Gibley even more was the fact that they had done it very effectively.

He looked round hoping to see a friendly face. He glanced up and saw the busy beavers in the Gallery. The Press! My God! How would they handle this?

Feeling miserable and ill, he shuffled out of the Chamber into the Members' Lobby. There he saw Archie Dundas surrounded by five of the Scottish Lobby Correspondents. But when Gibley appeared, they quickly broke off contact and made straight for him.

'Have you any statement to make on the exchange on Rossford Chemicals in the Chamber?' asked one of the lobby men, speaking for all five.

'No, I have not,' Gibley replied angrily. He was not in a mood to talk to this crowd of vultures, gathering for the kill. A wiser head would have taken the opportunity of speaking pleasantly. By a time-honoured tradition, which was scrupulously observed, Lobby Correspondents did not quote any comments made in the Lobby itself. This provided an opportunity of removing any misunderstandings arising out of speeches or questions in the House without the Member having to watch carefully each word he said.

But Gibley's head was not wise. It was aching. His only wish was to get a cup of coffee and escape from the scene of his humiliation.

He strode away from the Lobby correspondents, leaving them looking puzzled and, perhaps, amused.

As he entered the cafeteria, he remembered that he had not had any breakfast. So, as he moved along the counter with his tray, he purchased not only just his usual coffee, but also two of these splendid roll sandwiches which were so fatal for portly figures like his own.

Not wishing to engage in conversation, he grabbed three Scottish papers from the rack and sped towards a quiet corner.

'SHOCK FACTORY CLOSURE — 700 PAID OFF' screamed one headline. 'SCOTS LABOUR CHIEF SLAMS FACTORY SHUTDOWN' claimed another with the sub-heading 'Government Must Act to Save Jobs'.

So it was headline stuff. Gibley groaned. The luscious roll suddenly became tasteless and even offensive. How had the Labour so-and-so's been so quick off the mark? They must have had prior news from some of their Union friends. My goodness! There was his name at the foot of the page! Pulling the paper suddenly nearer his face as though he had seen his name in the Obituary column, Gibley read the paragraph.

'Mr. Gibley Horn, Tory M.P. for Rossford, was not available for comment last night' . . . that was a liberty! What they meant was that they could not find him because he was on the London–Glasgow train . . . 'but it was learned from Mr Alec Anderson, Conservative Agent for Rossford, that, although the subject was probably to be raised in the Commons this morning, Mr Horn was expected to be at his mansion in Rossford this morning and not in Parliament. "He usually comes up on the overnight train," Mr Anderson said late last night.'

He must speak to Alec Anderson about the Press, thought Gibley. He knew the form. A late phone call would have come to Alec's home, asking simply if Mr Horn would be home on Friday, as the Press would like to have a word with him. Ever anxious to please, Alec would just say 'Yes', and hence the story. He would take it up with Central Office about the *Star*. But they were terrified of upsetting the Press. What was the point?

But how on earth would they treat the Commons row? Without feeling any personal animosity towards the people of the East, Gibley thought how convenient it would be if there was a disastrous earthquake in Japan or a revolution in Thailand to fill up the front pages of the evening papers.

However, time was getting on. It was now almost noon. If he was to get that 2.30 p.m. plane and reach home in time to read up this television stuff, he would have to move. A bus out to the airport at 12.30—then a quick meal at the airport and then Glasgow before half past three. He would have to do well on television tonight. Very well indeed.

A quick taxi ride to the South Kensington Terminal enabled Gibley, still with his heavy case, to get his bus and he was in the Airport restaurant by 1.30. A quick glance through the London evening paper reassured him, because there was no mention of the Commons' storm! At least, it was not national news. But it was the Scottish ones that mattered. Nowhere in the paper was there any mention of that earthquake in Japan, or indeed of any other story, which might capture the headlines. In fact, Fleet Street appeared to be desperately short of news, the lead story being vague rumours of a rise in London bus fares.

Feeling a little better after his meal, although the bill was a shock, Gibley went along and booked a seat on the plane. So far so good. But, when he went to check in, the traffic clerk advised him with agreeable courtesy that there was a little technical trouble and the plane might be delayed.

'But I've got to get up to Glasgow immediately for a television performance!'

'We're doing everything possible to speed things up,' the clerk reassured him blandly.

But the clerk's optimism was ill-founded. One delay followed another, and before long it was after four o'clock.

Alarm seized him: the feeling of constriction in his chest intensified. Have to go direct to the studios now, he thought desperately. No time to get home or to read up that Party pamphlet. And he didn't know much about atomic power and all that stuff.

The first thing to do was to phone home. Margaret would be expecting him back by now. So he rummaged in his pocket for a shilling and dialled through.

'Rossford 2857.' Margaret sounded anxious.

'Hullo, dear. I'm still at London Airport. Technical delay,' he communicated the essential news in one breath.

'What's been happening in the House, Gibley?'

Margaret inquired apprehensively. 'There's a horrible story in the evening paper.'

'Tell you when I get home. Nothing to worry about.'

So it had been published. Wish it *was* nothing to worry about, Gibley thought darkly.

'But when will you be home?'

'I'll come straight from the Television Studios. Home about nine o'clock. The plane is being called now. Must fly.'

The plane was not being called but Gibley did not fancy a long conversation about this morning's troubles. Better to wait till he had time to think about it.

'But what about the pamphlet on Power?'

'Don't worry,' said Gibley. He always seemed to be telling Margaret not to worry. 'It's not important.'

'But you said it was this morning.'

'I've got all the information down here.' White lies of this sort were now so much a part of everyday life that Gibley knew that Margaret no longer paid any attention to them.

'I could always read it through and tell you the essential points over the phone.'

'No time, dear, Flight's being called. Cheerio. And don't worry!'

'Don't worry.' He was always saying that and it was never true.

Margaret was usually right. She should have been the M.P.!

By a happy coincidence, which eased his conscience somewhat, the voice came over the loudspeaker saying that Flight 186 to Glasgow was boarding now and, as he stepped along the gangway, the voice could still be heard making profuse apologies for the unavoidable delay and trusting that no inconvenience would be suffered by the passengers. If only they knew!

Now for another miserable air journey.

Oh no! Not *him*! There was the figure of Archie Dundas striding along just ahead of him. He must avoid sitting beside him at all costs. What was his seat number? C.1. Surely with so many seats available, Archie would not be C.2. Please no!

Fortunately, Archie was F.3 and Gibley was only required to exchange a rather hostile grunt of recognition with his Scottish colleague when their eyes met.

Hope his brandy chokes him! thought Gibley, and even enjoyed a little flutter of amusement at the picture conjured up in his mind of Archie spluttering and choking.

Having the window seat, Gibley hoped that his neighbour would not object to the blind being drawn. If he did not have to look outside, Gibley did not feel so nervous and he could reassure himself by stamping from time to time on the floor of the compartment to secure a sense of solidity which a sickening look down 20,000 feet certainly did not give him. But unfortunately his neighbour had important papers to read and needed all the light he could get. And when Gibley suggested that they might change seats, the gentleman declined in a huffy negative, clearly unaware that anyone could find it disagreeable to have to look out of the window. And so Gibley endured his usual spell of agony, finding his eyes drawn, despite his efforts, to the ground stretched out below him and waiting tensely for the bang, pop or ripping sound which would convey that the plane was out of control and that the passengers would have to make the journey down these 20,000 feet by the direct route. What a coward he must be, thought Gibley. The doctor had assured him that some people were just made that way. *He* certainly was.

At last they touched down safely at the Renfrew Airport and Gibley staggered off the plane. It was now 5.15. Only time to buy the Scottish evening papers, have a quick glance at them and collect his luggage.

As he lifted the papers off the kiosk counter, and was shocked to see his photo on both front pages, he spied the presence of Archie Dundas at his elbow, who commented in an unnecessarily loud voice: 'I see you're headline news today, Horn.' Realising that the people crowded round the kiosk were suddenly taking a great interest in him and would shortly realise that *he* was the idiot whose activities were spotlighted for the world to see for the price of fivepence, Gibley scurried away as fast as he could without seeming to lose his dignity.

He picked up his case and made for the car park where the old saloon was waiting faithfully. Safely installed within the privacy of his car he began to study the papers seriously.

'ROSSFORD M.P. IN COMMONS' STORM. ACCUSED OF WELCOMING 700 JOB LOSS.

'Amid angry scenes in the Commons today, Scots

Labour M.P.s bitterly accused Rossford M.P., Gibley Horn, of welcoming the closure of Rossford Chemicals' Manendon Factory which will make 700 unemployed. In fiery exchanges, the Rossford M.P.'s only contribution was to say that he "accepted the Minister's statement that the factory had to close". This produced uproar on the Labour benches and James McKinnon, Labour M.P. . . .'

As he read the story Gibley became acutely aware that two people were standing beside his car peering curiously through the windows, with evening papers in their hands.

He threw down the newspapers and pressed the self-starter angrily. As he drove out of the car park and sped along the road to the City Centre he suddenly realised that in forty minutes he would be discussing Power problems before an audience of over a million and, despite his turbulent state of mind, he racked his brain for any bits of information he had about the subject. But there was little to tap from that source. On every other subject he knew something. But not this one. Maybe, if the interviewer had a copy of the Tory pamphlet, and he almost certainly would, he could glance over it before going on the air.

Bump. Bump.

Not that, thought Gibley desperately. Not tonight of all nights. A flat tyre!

There was nothing to do but to get down to it. Rain had now started, but Gibley did not give this a thought. In a day of disasters, this seemed inevitable.

Every passing car seemed to take delight in sending a muddy spray over him while he toiled, and it was 5.45 before a miserable and mud-spattered Gibley Horn got back to the driving wheel.

Quarter of an hour to reach the studio. It was almost impossible to do so in the rush hour.

And impossible it proved to be. It was fully 6.10 p.m. when Gibley drove into the Studio car park and, waiting there to greet him, was an anxious little knot of men. As he got out of his car, they one and all took the opportunity of looking at their watches, as if to impress on the Rossford M.P. that he had kept the television men waiting and had wasted ten minutes of their very valuable time.

'Plane late. Flat tyre. So sorry.' Out blurted the excuses to an audience that was clearly in no mood to be impressed by them. 'I know time is short, but I must have a wash.'

Realising that talk took time, the cluster of telemen rushed Gibley along to a wash room and stood anxiously by, looking exasperated, as though nobody could take such a long time or be so akward in undertaking the simple task of washing.

The washing at last successfully completed, Gibley was hurried along to the studio where his two grim-faced Scottish Parliamentary colleagues were already seated in their chairs, whose positioning was precisely and clearly marked out in chalk on the floor.

After he had mumbled out his apologies, and exchanged pleasantries with the interviewer, Gibley settled down in his chair and the programme recording began.

✻✻✻ ✻✻✻ ✻✻✻

'Twenty seconds,' screamed one of the vast crowd of technicians dotted round the studio floor. It was just like a circus ring, during the final display, with the long-haired and exotic animals cavorting round. The only difference was that there was an audience of four.

'Ten seconds. Electricity. Atomic Power. Hydro-electricity. Mind a blank. Have to play this by ear.

'Five. Four. Three. Two. One.' With one second to go, one of the floor technicians, who appeared to have no other job, dramatically pulled down his arms which had been raised to the heavens as though he was exhorting the dignified performers to jump out of their seats and dive into fast cars for a race round the studio.

'Hallo again,' said the interviewer to the camera in that sweet and juicy manner which was uniquely his own, taking care to brush back an unruly lock of hair with a boyish gesture, thus exposing the full and unexpurgated features of his face to the multitude of admiring viewers.

'This is Dawson Donnelly here again to bring the drama of Westminster direct into your home.'

As if to emphasise the magnitude of this unique privilege which he was endowing, the studio lights went off and, to the accompaniment of martial music, Gibley found himself gazing at a procession of well-known Parliamentary scenes and figures flitting across the nearby screen.

'Another exciting week of drama in the House of Commons,' D.D. continued. And to provide proof of his contention he looked down eagerly at an assortment of papers delicately balanced on his knee.

Then looking straight at the 'idiot board' which was slowly turning above the camera to keep pace with his voice, he outlined the highlights of the week.

'On Monday, the Minister of Health came under attack from all quarters for what one Member described as "a lack of urgency in forward Health Service Planning".'

Lights out. More martial music. And on flashed the cheery confident face of the Minister himself looking as though he had the problems of forward planning well under control.

'Tuesday saw a dramatic and fierce debate on the Milk Marketing Board with both front benches accusing each other of being responsible for the cheese factory scandal which has been dominating this week's Press. Comment from Tom Wibley, Labour Spokesman on Agriculture—"The Minister is noted for his words and actions, but we have had too much of one and too little of the other".'

Again the lights flashed off with D.D. clearly in danger of doing himself an injury by laughing helplessly and uproariously at this gem of Parliamentary wit.

More music. Another face.

'On Thursday, we again had warning of new storms to come with Iain Constable, self-appointed leader of the Tory Left, cross-examining Sir Oliver about developments in the trouble-torn Amerbala Coastal Strip. Watch the nightly summary of next week's dramatic moves each night on this channel at eleven p.m. when we show you recorded highlights of the proceedings in the House. And, of course, your Friday Night "Big Ben Probe" with yours truly, Dawson Donnelly, in the chair.'

Glancing round hurriedly to confirm that none of the guests had dropped dead through exhaustion or excitement at this summary of the burdens which had rested on their shoulders during the week, and satisfied that all was well, he turned again to the camera.

'And this week the searchlight of "Big Ben Probe" falls on Power. Not political power. But the power which lights your homes, which turns the wheels of industry, which lights your streets at night, which cooks that luscious week-end joint. Electric power. And, to give their authoritative comments, we have in the studio Gibley Horn, Tory M.P. for Rossford, just back from London where this morning he battled with Labour M.P.s protesting about the closure of Rossford Chemicals' Manendon Factory.'

Pause. Camera 3 direct on to Gibley's puzzled and portly face.

'David Mason, Labour M.P. for Lanark Central, and a top Opposition spokesman on power problems.'

Another pause while Davie looked dignified and nodded a pleasant 'Good Evening' to the invisible audience.

'From the North, carrying the Liberal banner, we have William Grierson, a Westminster new boy serving a far from silent apprenticeship.'

'Well, new M.P.s should be seen and heard,' Grierson interrupted jocularly in one of these impromptu flashes of chattiness which endeared him to viewers.

As Gibley Horn alone had been silent to date and as, in the rush, no voice-level tests had been taken, D.D. decided to bring him in straight away in case a bad speech performance would require a re-take. Better not, he thought grimly. This would mean an entire new introduction.

'The most important development in "power" politics has been the publication of the Barron Report.'

Heard of that, thought Gibley, but what in earth was it about? Must listen for a clue.

'What do Scots M.P.s think of its content and implications?

'Gibley Horn,' D.D. pounced, making it clear that the first reaction must come from him.

Panic.

'Well,' said Gibley, immediately regretting his opening inasmuch as, at the Central Office television school, he remembered being told that 'Well' gave the immediate impression of lack of confidence and absence of factual information. How right they were!

'Well. This is a most important Report with wide-reaching implications.' That was always a safe start. 'As you know, the Government has a splendid record in electricity supply and has spent many millions on capital schemes.'

He remembered the Central Office fellow saying that they had a good record.

'I think that the report is right in emphasising the

huge demand for power, and I am confident that with
the combined contribution of atomic power, hydro-
electric power and conventional electrical generating
stations we have *every* reason to look forward with
confidence.'

That wasn't bad. He had covered up his total
although, he hoped, temporary ignorance of this
Barron Report and the conversation which followed
should make it clear what specific proposals, if any,
the Barron Report had contained.

But the look of astonishment on D.D.'s face conveyed
forcibly that perhaps Gibley had not been entirely
successful and Davie Mason's sharp retort removed any
doubts.

'We know that Mr Horn has had a trying day in the
Commons,' he started with a smirk, 'but, even allowing for this, I find his comments incomprehensible.'
He said 'incomprehensible', but the look on his face
conveyed forcibly that he had encountered an example
of absolute folly and ignorance when he had been
expecting only a minor impairment of mental facul-
ties.

'I wonder if Mr Horn has ever read the Report? It
deals, as *you* know, Mr Donnelly, with natural gas
production and the consequences which this will have
on electricity. Mr Horn is right in one thing: the
Government is pouring millions of pounds into capital
schemes in atomic power, hydro-electric power, conventional electricity generating stations, but the point
the Report makes is that the Government might well
have been pouring this hard-earned taxpayers' money

right down the drain in face of vast cheaper sources of power supply from natural gas.'

It was now Bill Grierson's turn.

'I don't blame Mr Horn *entirely* for not having read the Report, because we have so many papers to read as Members of Parliament. However, surely, as one of the Scottish Tory Members, he might have tried to read a document of such vital concern to Scotland.'

Having driven Davie Mason's point home in a courteous but much more telling way, he turned to the positive side.

'The Liberal Party has always supported the harnessing of the most modern and economic power supplies to ensure economic growth, but at all times this must be subject to social considerations.'

He paused, briefly allowing a short while for the television audience to reflect that Liberals cared for people.

'This in Scotland means the welfare of the many thousands of enthusiastic workers, technicians and managers who have devoted their lives to this great industry. We cannot expect them to bear the full brunt of massive errors of judgment on the part of the Government.'

This was disastrous, thought Gibley, but there was still time to put things right.

'You don't need to read hundreds of Reports to realise the importance of North Sea gas,' he countered. 'We should remember that it is private enterprise which is giving us this wonderful new cheap source of energy, and if we had listened to the Labour Party some years ago, it might have gone the same way as other nationalised industries—higher prices and a raw deal for the consumer!'

Splendid, he congratulated himself. And he waited eagerly for Mason's reply to that formidable onslaught.

He did not have to wait long.

'I'm beginning to think we should adjourn this programme to let Mr Horn read the Barron Report,' he said impatiently, 'as we are talking at cross-purposes. The whole point of the Report was that the composition of North Sea gas limited its effective use to replacing conventional gas, but that natural gas transported in liquid form from Africa' —he emphasised Africa to ensure that even someone of Gibley's limited intelligence could grasp its significance— 'could be processed to produce cheaper supplies of electricity. I may add that the Labour Party is more than aware of the potentialities of this development and, while fully accepting Grierson's point about social priorities, we think that the vast increase in bulk transportation of liquid gas in Africa could stimulate many orders for the Scottish shipyards which have been so shockingly neglected by this Government.'

Ships! Gibley thought desperately. I know something about that. Here we go again.

'What nonsense about the shipyards. I visited one Clyde Yard recently and they are full of confidence about the future. They've invested a great deal in new machines and this particular Yard has enough work for three years.'

'A typical Tory reaction,' replied Davie Mason. 'Mr Horn will no doubt not have asked about the men who work in the shipyards. Perhaps he doesn't know that, while his Director friends have been buying their wonderful new machines and no doubt making good profits, five thousand shipyard jobs have disappeared in Scotland? In the Clyde area alone, the numbers employed have fallen by twenty per cent in three years. This may be Tory prosperity, but it's not my idea of progress.'

Feeling that he had been pushed out of the conversation, Grierson stepped in.

'Speaking as a Northern M.P., I am acutely concerned, as are my constituents, about the future of hydro-electric power stations. We have little enough employment up there, and if the jobs of hydro-workers are going to be affected as a result of a scandalous "boob" by the Tory Government, we will fight this all the way.'

Grierson had heard that redundancies were inevitable and was anxious at this stage to apportion blame, lest any of the electorate might think that their champion at Westminster was in any way responsible. Shame that this programme does not go up to the far North, he reflected, but he would get a transcript of the broadcast and give it to the local Press.

In a last desperate effort to restore his position, Gibley grabbed at a straw of information he remembered from election time.

'But it was the Conservative Government which spent large sums of money on hydro-electric schemes,' he proclaimed. 'It was the last Labour Government which cancelled the forward schemes up there, and I hope that the Highlands will remember this.'

'While not accepting for one minute Mr Horn's praise for Tory Highland policies—and if he has any doubts he should go up there and see for himself—the Barron Report confirms that it would have been criminal to spend vast amounts of money on power stations when cheaper power could be found elsewhere. Much better to spend the money on jobs which will last and not simply disappear as a result of Government incompetence.'

'And last word from William Grierson,' chipped in D.D., quite pleased at the way the programme had gone—good punchy stuff, despite this Tory thickhead.

'The Barron Report is a most important one for Scotland,' Grierson said in a New Statesmanlike manner, knowing that the interviewer's interruption would prevent any comment on his summing-up, 'and Scottish M.P.s of all parties will have to watch developments with vigilance to ensure that the interests of the nation are not neglected as they have been, too often, in the past.'

'Well, there you have it for another week,' said D.D., 'and don't forget to tune in to "Big Ben Probe" next Friday when, assuming no unforeseen developments, we will be probing the housing crisis in our cities. Good night.'

Off went the lights, the M.P.s and the interviewer remaining still and silent, three from the discipline which previous studio participation produced and

Gibley Horn through the paralytic effect of sheer misery.

More silence.

'Thank you, studio,' shrieked the floor manager and immediately babbling confusion broke out.

'And thank you, gentlemen,' said D.D.

'Hope you can come into the viewing room to see a recording of the programme with refreshments supplied by courtesy of the studio before you rush home to see your smiling faces on the tele at ten o'clock.'

Davie Mason and Bill Grierson stepped smartly towards the viewing room hardly able to hide their willingness to see the results of their triumphant performance. And poor Gibley shuffled along behind them, fully conscious that most of the eyes in the studio were on him.

'I'm afraid that I wasn't as well prepared as I would have liked to be,' he mumbled to D.D. 'Don't suppose there's any chance of a retake?'

The understatement of the year, thought D.D. inwardly, but outwardly he assured Mr Horn pleasantly that this would not be possible.

For one thing, the studios were fully booked and "Big Ben Probe" had exceeded its recording time with Gibley's late arrival. He also anticipated a little difficulty in persuading Messrs Mason and Grierson of the desirability of a further recording when Gibley Horn might be more effective having grasped, by now, the essential points of the Barron Report.

Not the slightest bit surprised at the other M.P.s having taken advantage of his position and, indeed, having a feeling that he had in some way let the side down, Gibley apologised to his colleagues as he had done to D.D.

They were most understanding and sympathetic about the treatment which he had received in the House that morning.

'Archie Dundas *is* rather a tiresome fellow,' Davie Mason whispered to Gibley confidentially.

And Bill Grierson said cheerily: 'I really did mean that piece about how impossible it was to read all these reports. I don't think the public have any idea of the work we M.P.s do.'

Peace, friendship and gin were lavishly distributed and harmony signed until the recording was played back.

Gibley was appalled. If he sounded bad, he looked worse! Hesitant, unsure of facts, pompous, at times unintelligible. And he hurried speedily from the scene of his indignity, leaving the three behind—no doubt to have a jolly gossip about him.

The rain was now pouring down, and with difficulty he made home by 8.15 p.m.

As he stepped into his house, he felt like bursting into tears and collapsing into his wife's arms in a desperate search for sympathy. As he embraced her, the phone rang.

'Oh dear,' said Margaret, conscious of the need to protect Gibley from further troubles in what had been a depressing day. 'It will be these Press men; they've been on the phone most of the night. Shall I say you're not at home?'

'I'll answer it.' He was anxious to save his wife from hearing yet another account of the morning's episode from a newspaperman.

But it was not the Press. It was his Chairman, Major Anthony Perkins. He sounded brusque and irritable.

'Glad I caught you. Terrible Press story in the Evenings. You'll have to issue a statement or something. Some of the Club members were very critical tonight. It doesn't do the Party any good.'

Gibley started to explain what had happened, but he was cut short.

'No time for that just now,' said the Major impatiently. 'I was coming back from the Club for dinner and saw a big crowd at that tenement in Rossford High Street at the corner of Baker Street. Beside the pub,' he added to identify the locus more exactly. 'The foundations have gone all twisted with this rain and the police are warning the people to get out. Loads of Press men around. Think you had better get down there right away and show an interest.'

It was impossible to argue with the Major when he was in one of these bullying moods and started to talk of the Party: and Baker Street was only ten minutes away. A slight shiver ran up his spine.

He outlined the emergency to Margaret.

'But I've got your meal all ready in the oven.' She almost wailed, 'you *must* stop for a while or you'll have a heart attack. Why not go down after dinner?'

But it was one of these days! Gibley knew that if he waited the building would probably collapse while he

4

was enjoying his dinner and the Major would be on to him again.

So off he drove again, in the pouring rain, to offer sympathy to the tenants of Tayworth Buildings in the High Street.

There was a big crowd when he arrived.

'Shocking,' said one bystander, 'should have been pulled down years ago.'

Gibley was usually at his best in such emergencies and he pushed his way through the crowd, rather more confidently after someone said in a stage whisper: 'There's the M.P.!'

As he approached the building, which was already looking a little lop-sided, he was stopped by a fresh-faced constable.

'Can't go in there. It's dangerous.'

Explaining that he was the Parliamentary representative of the unfortunate inhabitants, Gibley then inquired as to their fate. Most of them, it appeared, had been taken to the Welfare Home in Morrison Place.

Knowing that he would have to go there to see the families, Gibley looked round to see if he could spy the crowds of reporters whom the Major had assured him would be present to take down the M.P.'s condolences and assurances of action. But the only person he recognised was Jackie Mulholland, the sole reporter on the staff of the *Rossford Gazette*.

'And where are the rest of your Press colleagues?'

There was no point in pouring out his heart to the representative of this local rag and then having to repeat it again to the others.

He learned from the youngster that they had departed, after taking some pictures, to write up copy for the first editions of the following morning's papers. Others had made for the Welfare Home. Splendid. He might get there before they left. And so, after murmuring the usual sympathetic noises to the *Gazette* man, Gibley marched back to his car and made for the grim Welfare Home through the rain and darkness.

There were several cars outside, so it seemed that he was in time. He opened the front door of the Home and stepped into the hallway. There, a crowd of newsmen were gathered round some bedraggled-looking men and women who were speaking angrily and pointing with feeling at a grubby paper one of them held in his hand.

'Talk of the devil,' whispered the *Star* reporter to one of his colleagues and jerking his thumb in the direction of the door where our Rossford M.P. was providing a generous contribution of rain water to the Home's well-polished floor, as he stood there dripping.

'My name's Horn,' he announced. 'I'm the local M.P. and I've called to offer my sympathy and help.' He stepped towards the cluster of people.

'We know you fine well,' answered a member of the crowd, clearly having left his collar, his tie and his good manners in his sinking home at Tayworth Buildings.

'We remember *you*, but do *you* mind this letter?' He shoved the grubby paper into Gibley's face. The latter read it quickly, having had enough misunderstanding for one day.

'Dear Mr Thomson,' he read. It was a letter. One of his own.

'I refer to our conversation in my Committee Rooms about the housing conditions which you and your neighbours are experiencing. I have been in touch with the authorities and am glad to say that you and your neighbours at 489 High Street should all be re-housed before the end of the year and the property closed for demolition. I am glad that I have been able to help.'

Gibley looked at the letter helplessly. There at the foot was his own splendid signature. Looking at Mr Thomson's angry face he remembered the details.

This fellow had come to his interview session over a year ago about his house and this had prompted the M.P. to write to the Town Clerk. Back had come a reply saying that the Health Department had the property under constant surveillance and that their plans were to have the people re-housed soon, almost certainly before the end of the year.

'I wouldn't have written this without the Council confirming it. They must have altered their plans.'

'Pass the buck,' said one angry voice.

'All promises,' said another. 'And we got it from you just before the Election.' 'Is that how you earn your sixty-five pounds a week?'

'That's most unfair,' protested Gibley.

Another, younger, figure made his way forward. 'First you do me out of my job,' he shouted angrily, 'and now I'm in the street after you promised us a new house months ago. I'm going to see a lawyer.'

'Your job?' Gibley inquired with disbelief written all over his face.

'I work for Rossford Chemicals,' came the explanation.

The evicted tenants had had a wretched evening. They were cold, wet, miserable and without a home. Somebody must be to blame. Here was the scapegoat delivered into their hands!

The conversation grew heated and an agitated Gibley Horn was conscious of flash bulbs popping all round him.

No matter how he tried to explain his position, it was of no avail and he eventually decided to depart when one rather burly gentleman offered to punch his nose through his bloody face. His scraggy wife hovered by his side, looking as though she would take pleasure in inflicting further grisly injuries.

The reporters crowded round Gibley outside the door and all he could say to them, honestly, was that the Council would have to provide the answer to the enigma about the new houses.

As a sad and soaking M.P. drove back to his home, the *Star* Office was already receiving its story.

'Just back from a Commons storm in which angry Labour M.P.s accused him of welcoming the closure of the major Rossford Chemical Factory, Rossford's Tory M.P. faced another storm in his constituency. Pathetic crowds of tenants, removed by the police from their sinking homes in High Street, Rossford, confronted the 56-year-old M.P. with a letter they had received from him just before the last Election promising them new homes quote before the end of the year unquote.'

'Mr Fred Thomson, who with his wife and three

young children had to abandon his furniture and clothing in his home as police rushed them from their two apartment house said, angrily, quote We've all been fooled. The M.P.'s letter isn't worth the paper it's written on. He's been making political profit out of our misery end quote. The Rossford M.P. first denied knowledge of the letter and then, when confronted with it, placed the blame on the shoulders of the Council. Commenting on Mr Horn's accusation, Rossford Health Chief, Augustus Plummer, said that the Burgh's plans for demolishing property had been delayed by Government curbs on spending and he said that he was surprised that Mr Horn had been so definite in his letter knowing how plans could be upset by Government financial policy. End story. Picture of Horn and angry tenants follows with letter to tenants for copy and reproduction. Check story for libel.'

And within two hours the great rollers in the *Star* office were churning out newspapers with this splendid headline splash.

It was 9.45 before Gibley got back home and, as he expected, the 'gentlemen of the Press' had been ringing constantly to seek his comments on the Chemical Factory story and later on the Tayworth Buildings row.

'Surely not *more* trouble,' said Margaret. 'What's all this about these poor tenants and some letter you wrote?'

'Let's have a meal and I'll tell you about it,' said Gibley weakly.

'It'll be ruined,' said Margaret in a hurt voice. And then quickly capturing her sense of priorities she shouted through from the kitchen, 'Quick. Put on the television, your programme will just be coming on.'

The phone rang again at that point and soon the curtain came down on a disastrous day.

❋❋❋　❋❋❋　❋❋❋

After a more or less sleepless night, Gibley wakened at 9 a.m. During the night, when he had lain awake, he had tried to persuade himself that the previous day had just been a nightmare. And, during his spasms of sleep, he had dreamed constantly of rushing through a railway station on a hot summer's day with his heavy coat and bowler on, carrying two loaded suitcases, desperately trying to catch a train which was always just pulling out as he rushed along the platform.

Margaret was already downstairs thinking only about how she was going to face the next week as the Member of Parliament's wife. What on earth would she say to the ladies at the Coffee Morning and what would they say to her? With Gibley's antics blazoned abroad it was as if her husband was the local clergyman and had been arrested by the police for standing in the public square without his trousers and knocking a constable's hat off with a beer bottle. Gibley would soon be back in London, but she had to stay and face the music at home in the constituency. Late the previous night she had managed to get some idea of the day's events, but the morning papers delivered through her door had shown that even her husband's gloomy descriptions had been a serious underestimate.

The more immediate problem was the West Church Women's Auxiliary Bazaar. She would have to go with her husband and it promised to be the most embarrassing experience up to date. Those who had not read their evening and morning papers would have seen the deplorable television performance and that minority who were both blind and deaf would not be at the Bazaar in sufficient numbers to occupy her attention for the afternoon. And then, she had to provide dinner for Major and Mrs Perkins. How much better if her husband had been a humble shopkeeper or a coalman without the complications and cruelty of this political life. Was it still too late to get out? She sometimes wondered. And could they escape to a less tormenting existence?

As Gibley came downstairs for breakfast the telephone rang.

'I can't take any more,' he cried in desperation. 'Tell them I've eloped to Tibet with the Prime Minister's wife. Anything at all. But I'm not at home!'

Margaret answered the phone, looking tearful. It soon became clear that the call was for her and not for Gibley.

'Of course we'll still be coming to the Bazaar,' he heard her saying. 'Gibley is quite well, thank you, and I know he's looking forward to the afternoon.'

'Who was that?' Gibley asked, knowing fine well that it was the Chairman of the West Church Women's Auxiliary but anxious nevertheless to find out how the land lay.

'It was just Mrs Hamilton of the Women's Auxiliary.

Anxious to know if you would still be opening their Bazaar this afternoon after what she referred to as "these horrible newspapermen",' she concluded with a touch of sarcasm.

They had a silent breakfast, both deep in thought.

The hush was broken by Gibley, who said with feeling, 'You know I'm desperately sorry for landing you in all this, Margaret. I'm really fed up with it. What about chucking it and running some small hotel up North where nobody knows us and getting away from these beastly politicians and reporters?'

'It would have to be Tibet if we were to get away from everyone who knew us,' said his wife wearily. 'But I'm getting more than a little sick of it all myself. This constant phone. And it's not doing your health any good with this rushing up and down, to and from London.'

'But what would we do for money?'

It was the old problem.

'If I save like mad,' said Gibley, 'and if Parliament goes on for another three years or so, I could have wiped out the overdraft and built up the deposit for a small hotel.'

I wonder, thought Margaret. She had ceased to feel optimistic about anything.

They had always been 'saving like mad', but the money went out all the same.

Anxious not to destroy entirely her husband's new-found enthusiasm, she suggested helpfully, 'I suppose that we could clear about £1,500 from the house after paying off the bond.'

'At least that,' Gibley chirped, always the optimist. 'Maybe as much as £2,500.'

Grasping at this small ray of hope, he squared his shoulders and walked out to the hall to pick up his brief-case in preparation for his interview session which was to start at ten o'clock in the basement of the Conservative Club, just off the High Street.

'Do try and get back by noon,' called his wife. 'We have to get ready for the Bazaar.'

'Do my best,' said Gibley, 'not many electors will want to consult an idiot like me.'

But the public were all-forgiving, particularly when they sought favours free and without charge. When he arrived at the Club, the steward informed him that ten people were already in the waiting-room anxious to have the benefit of his advice.

'First, please,' he called, as he passed through the waiting-room.

The first case was an unusual one. Miss McGlinchy had seen a splendid advertisement for a fine new form of water heater. She had filled in the questionnaire and sent a fourpenny stamp on the basis of the firm's assurance that there was no obligation of any sort. He suspected that the old girl had sent in the form just to get a letter through the post. Terrible thing, this loneliness. Must send a letter to Margaret next week from London. She'll be feeling pretty low. Always used to do it in the old days, but you know how it is.

'And the next week a man came in a big car and said that, if I gave him a pound and filled in a request form, he could arrange for one to be brought out

without commitment and let me see how it worked,'
related Miss McGlinchy.

'Then the next day I got another letter,' Miss
McGlinchy explained with a certain pride, 'thanking
me for my order and saying that the heater would be
installed the next week. Well, as I said, I hadn't
ordered *anything* at all.'

'But what did the request form say, Miss McGlinchy?'
Gibley inquired.

'I'm sure that I don't know. The man distinctly said
that it was just a request form.'

It seemed that, when the heater had been installed,
Miss McGlinchy had had second thoughts and she
immediately wrote a letter saying thank you very much
for the trial but could they please take it away and
could she have her pound back? Predictably, all that
she received in reply was a sharp letter demanding
payment within seven days. And further stern demands
followed.

'Can you get me my pound back, Mr Oswald?'

'Horn,' he corrected her. 'Mr Oswald was the M.P.
before me. He died five years ago.'

'What a shame!' Miss McGlinchy looked very sad
indeed. 'And what is your name?'

'Horn. H—O—R—N.' Gibley spelled out the name
carefully, hoping that she would remember it when she
next had to visit the Polling Station.

But Miss McGlinchy did not appear to be impressed
and simply took the opportunity to recall the old
political figures whom she remembered or whom her
father had admired.

'Bonar Law,' she recalled from her vast store of political memories. 'I mind my father saying, "that chap will be Prime Minister some day". And so he did,' Miss McGlinchy confirmed, lest Gibley's knowledge was in any way inadequate.

Desperately trying to impress the old lady with the relative seriousness of her position with the water-heater suppliers, Gibley eventually undertook to write to the Company and ask for her to be released from her obligations.

Try as she could, Miss McGlinchy could not remember the name of the firm. But she had it at home. And she would write to Mr Horn when she got home and he could write back to her from the House of Commons. So Miss McGlinchy departed, pleased with her interview with this nice new M.P., and not at all depressed at the prospect of receiving a letter from the House of Commons. This would make her week and provide added pleasure to Mrs Smith in the grocer's shop and Mr McGrory in the newsagents, both of whom would be privileged to see the letter which little Miss McGlinchy had received from the Palace of Westminster.

When Miss McGlinchy had gone, Gibley called the next customer and was rather alarmed to see that around fifteen constituents were now in the waiting-room, all looking decidedly annoyed at what they regarded as the excessive time which Gibley had spent with the old lady.

'Won't keep you a minute,' announced the next caller, a middle-aged man who conducted himself with a military precision. That was a relief.

'Just want to protest strongly about the activities of those fellow-traveller Tory M.P.s who criticise our troops in the Amerbala Coastal Strip. Thousands think like me. All the chaps in the office. Go and see your M.P., I said. And here I am. Well, the United Nations can go to blazes. That's what I say. Crowd of savages themselves, many of them. We should shoot that Dr Iffenzi. That's what I say. Not put him up at a first-class hotel in the Seychelles!'

Gibley hastened to assure this expert in international affairs that his views on Amerbala were quite orthodox and that he would back Sir Oliver to the last Gurkha. After a further brief discussion, in the course of which they exchanged a series of criticisms of the emergent nations in the Afro-Asian bloc, this outward-looking constituent and his tightly-rolled umbrella marched in unison out the door.

Next came a lady hoping for a council house, and all Gibley could do was offer to send a nice letter to the Town Clerk and to forward on to her the inevitable nice refusal which would follow two weeks later.

Then there was a National Assistance case. Sorry, not National Assistance any more, but it was the same old office in Flowers Crescent and the old lettering could still be seen through the thin paint which was probably sold to the Ministry as top-quality gloss.

Mr Sorenson was unemployed with a strained muscle, no doubt the result of swinging the lead for many years. The Ministry had taken £2 off his Benefit and he wanted it back pronto. If Mr Horn would do nothing about it, he was going to write to Sir Oliver.

If the latter refused to act, he would send a letter to the Queen. And if the Queen was too busy with other things, he would take the ultimate step of writing to the *Star*.

Mr Sorenson might have been a little more tactful than to mention the *Star* that morning of all mornings. The M.P. huffily explained that 'Wages Stop' was not a Tory plot to steal his hard-earned benefit, but simply a means of ensuring that people could not get more money from the Ministry benefit than they would get when working. Otherwise, there would be no incentive for anyone to get better quickly and return to work. But Mr Sorenson denied the need for any such incentive and departed in wrath mumbling incoherently about his rights; no doubt intent on commencing the long series of correspondence which would lead him through Downing Street and Buckingham Palace to the guardians of liberty and justice at *Star House*.

Next came Mrs Allison who had a problem with drains. Gibley was pleased to hear that her factor was Angus McPherson, an old school friend, and he was able to assure her, with some confidence, that her problem would be a temporary one.

After five interviews ranging over the more usual problems of pensions, housing, schools, vandalism and emigration, Gibley received a gentleman who showed the importance of his mission by peering anxiously round the cupboard to make sure that no spies were present. As he sat down on the hard wooden chair which Gibley had installed to discourage callers of undue length, he took the opportunity of having a glance under the table to convince himself that the midget spies, which hostile powers were no doubt recruiting for just such a purpose, were not lurking beneath it.

'Can I speak to you in confidence, Mr Horn?' he inquired anxiously, at the same time seeking to hide a substantial carton marked 'Creamed Rice' behind his insignificant person

'Of course,' Gibley replied, knowing that he was probably in for some light relief. He could spot these types a mile away, although it became a little tiresome if they kept calling. The object of the interview from his point of view must be solely to ensure that the gentleman would not come again.

The box, Mr Smith (as the visitor declared his name to be) assured him, was a submarine computer decimator which he had designed himself and manufactured in his loft. All Russian submarines, he informed Gibley in whispers, had computers aboard. And by sending out beams from his box which would home on the nearest submarine, he could make the computer go haywire and the submarine would blow up. He had written to the Admiralty and to the Prime Minister, but apart from a visit from a policeman nothing had happened.

Gibley Horn nodded sympathetically and looked suitably surprised that the highest powers in the Executive should pay such scant attention to so major a technical achievement.

Anticipating the first and most obvious question, Mr Smith continued in secretive whispers:

'I've knocked out fifteen already. But the Russians have hushed the whole thing up. Not a word in the papers. Crafty devils.'

Pulling out the box with a flourish in a demonstration to convince Mr Horn that the carton did not contain creamed rice, he produced a plastic box which looked rather like a miniature sewing-machine with a handle sticking out of the side.

He twisted round a knob, which had clearly seen better days on an electric cooker, until it showed the figure 500 degrees—and Very Hot, and another to the figure 4. After a little pause he proceeded to turn the handle furiously.

Then he sat back in his chair and, giving the box a friendly pat, said gleefully, 'That's another of the blighters gone.' The frenzied giggles and sniggers which poured out of Mr Smith gave Gibley time to ponder.

'Quite remarkable,' Gibley stated. 'But where do you stay, Mr Smith?'

'In Manendon,' came the reply from the now-exhausted Mr Smith who seemed pleased, nevertheless, to have impressed the M.P.

'My God!' Gibley gasped. 'That's not my constituency. You shouldn't have told me all this. Mr Dundas is your M.P.—Mr Archibald Dundas. You live outside my area and I shouldn't have heard about these secrets. However, I promise you that I will forget every word you've told me, Mr Smith.' (This, in any event, was at least true.) 'And you must not tell Mr Dundas that you have been to see me.

Looking up a little blue book and mumbling 'Security Index', Gibley scribbled down Archie Dundas's home address on a plain piece of paper and said, in a whisper, 'That's where Mr Dundas lives. Go and see him. And, remember, not a word about our talk.'

Pulling open the door and peering hastily into the waiting-room, apparently looking to see if any Russian spies had slipped in, he whispered to Mr Smith, 'Quick, it's safe to go now.'

Mr Smith scurried out clutching Archie Dundas's security address. And as Gibley listened patiently to a tale of woe from his next caller, he could not help thinking about the pleasant surprise which was about to interrupt Archie Dundas's week-end. Perhaps, he thought, just as he was starting his dinner!

In all, he saw twenty-one constituents that day, and not one of them mentioned anything about the happenings of Friday. This gave Gibley more confidence to face the world. But it was past one o'clock when he left the Club and he remembered in a panic that he had to change and get to the West Church Bazaar in time for the opening at 2.30 p.m.

✻✻✻   ✻✻✻   ✻✻✻

'You're quite hopeless, Gibley,' said Margaret, looking fiercely at the clock which was racing round to fill the air with the chimes of half past one.

'Your lunch is on the table, but help me to zip this up before you start.'

Her worried frown showed that she had worse things on her mind than the simple pressures of time. Because, of course, nobody likes to have a husband making a public idiot of himself and fewer still could obtain any satisfaction from having a husband whose activities were plastered over the Press when he did so. The situation might have been tolerable if Gibley could be hidden from the world within 'Beechgrove's' high walls for a week or so until other dramatic happenings pushed the story of yesterday into the cloudier reels of history. But it was a bit much to be forced to parade him publicly at the West Church Bazaar the day after the embarrassing events we have recorded.

'And try not to spend too much at the Bazaar. There's *never* anything we want there. My cupboards are full of useless stuff. I just hope that none of them recognise those tea cosies when they appear again at the Conservative Fête. Five pounds or so is quite enough.'

'Money! My God!' Gibley panicked. He had come up in the overnight train on Thursday night with fifteen pounds in his pocket specifically set aside for the Bazaar and the week-end's activities. But the journey of yesterday—the £4 taxi ride, the meals, the parking charges, the newspapers, the airport buses, the drinks —these must have eaten into his financial resources.

He pulled out his wallet and rummaged through it. Two pound notes, one ten-shilling note. There must be a mistake! But there wasn't! This was all he had. And a search of his pocket revealed only 3/5½d.

What an idiot he was! But no need to tell Margaret

until it was absolutely necessary. Perhaps he would not need to tell her at all.

'How are you off for money?' he shouted up the stairs.

'Cleaned out,' the reply wafted downwards and Gibley's heart sank even further. 'Must go to the bank first thing on Monday. Leave me out two or three pounds. Make it three. I will have to buy some rubbish too.'

'I'm afraid that won't be possible,' Gibley muttered, preferring to break the news at a distance.

'Stop mumbling,' his wife shouted, clearly not having picked up the message. 'I'll be down in a second.'

By the time she came, Gibley had laid the three notes and the 3/5½d down on the table beside his half-eaten dinner.

This visual treat and the brief explanation which accompanied it informed Margaret of the latest emergency in a few moments.

'Oh, no!' came the hopeless comment. 'Well, write out a cheque for five pounds and we'll spend the cash as sparingly as we can.'

But this was not a solution. He had been meaning to send for a new cheque-book all week, but time had been against him. Normal people faced with such an emergency could have borrowed from the neighbours, but 'Beechgrove' did not have any neighbours in the accepted sense and, in any event, M.P.s could not reasonably indulge in such a performance. It would be gossiped round the neighbourhood in a few days.

'We'll have to call it off,' Margaret cried in desperation. 'You're ill. Remember that.'

Gibley was more than willing to co-operate with this proposal and sat in a chair looking sick while his wife dialled the number of Mrs Hamilton, convener of the Bazaar, to convey the sad news that her husband was suddenly indisposed. But there was no response from the Hamilton home. Clearly they had taken off for the West Church and were no doubt waiting patiently for the arrival of the M.P. and his loaded coffers. A call to the Manse to pass the news to the Minister's wife was equally unsuccessful.

'It's five past two. We'll have to go. Make the best of it. Let's go.'

And so the pair sped off in silence to the West Church. Gibley had opened so many of these sales that he no longer prepared a speech. He usually gathered his thoughts during the journey, but instead he was thinking out his own 'feeding the five thousand' problem, of how £2 13s 5½d could be effectively distributed round the many stalls which the ladies of the Women's Auxiliary would have been preparing for throughout the long winter's nights.

The exercise in frugal spending might have been an easier task for someone used to counting pennies, but the Rossford M.P. had a free-spending nature and he tended to let go even those restraints which he normally had, when he opened sales of work.

'Fifteen and threepence?' he would inquire with apparent disbelief, 'for this lovely tea cosy,' holding up a grotesque knitted article in three glaring colours.

'Yes, I must have this for my good lady. No change.
Certainly not—just a small donation.' And so he would
endear himself to the ladies who spent the long winter
evenings making these objects and fire them with
enthusiasm to perpetrate further artistic outrages
during the next winter as well. But today the hard-
working ladies of the West Church Women's Auxiliary
would have to look elsewhere for such inspiration.

'Welcome indeed, Mr Horn,' the dog-collared
gentleman greeted Gibley, 'and a warm West Church
welcome to you also, dear Mrs Horn.'

Gibley grinned politely to the extent to which his
honest poverty would permit and, after exchanging
polite handshakes with the Committee, the party
moved towards the platform which was decorated with
artificial flowers and a handful of ladies clutching
shopping baskets. As always, Mrs Horn's hat was an
object of greater interest than the M.P. himself and
Gibley felt indebted to Margaret for providing this
diversion to distract attention from himself.

But soon the attention of the hall was directed to the
Minister, as he rose out of the hard wooden seat which
had provided a fleeting resting-place for his substantial
frame on the gay platform. Even the larger number of
ladies standing at the stalls with hands hovering over
the more desirable purchases, ready to pounce as soon
as the magic word 'Open' was said, turned slightly,
without surrendering their tactical position.

'Good afternoon, ladies and gentlemen, and blessing
on you this sunny afternoon,' he began enthusiastically.
'And congratulations to the ladies of the Women's

Auxiliary who have worked so hard to produce such lovely items for you to buy at this Bazaar in aid of the Dry Rot Fund.'

A topical joke came to Gibley's mind. Get them laughing and they might not notice the lack of spending so much.

'And, to perform the official opening ceremony, we have our very good friend and Member of Parliament, and we are delighted that he has brought with him his charming wife.' This produced a ripple of applause.

'I have now much pleasure in introducing to you, although he needs no introduction to a Rossford audience, Mr Gibley Horn, M.P.'

There was no applause as the M.P. stood up to address the gathering. This did not necessarily imply hostility, because Bazaar audiences generally believe that the opener of the function should complete his performance before he earned his supper of applause.

'Good afternoon, ladies and gentlemen, and thank you very much for your kind reception.' This sounded a bit daft as there had been no reception at all, friendly or hostile, but Gibley always began this way.

'I must first offer my congratulations to the Committee and the Women's Guild at the wonderful display we have before us.'

'Auxiliary,' the Minister corrected him in a stage whisper.

There was no doctrinal significance in the terminology, but accuracy was a virtue much appreciated by the occupant of the Manse.

Taking no notice of this interruption, Gibley continued:

'And I hope that you will all give very generously as it is a very good cause—the Dry Rot Fund. I know a lot about dry rot,' he said seriously, intending to give a short account of the troubles at 'Beechgrove', but he was blown a little off course by a comment from one of the audience—'Thinking of his speeches?'—and he glowered in the direction of the unwelcome heckler. The gentleman in question had not intended to be discourteous, but this was too good an opportunity for a man of his wit to miss. A few coarse laughs showed that the jest had conveyed its message.

'I know all about dry rot,' Gibley repeated, looking very flustered, but only making the position a lot worse. 'My wife complained about the dry rot at "Beechgrove" over a year ago and we cut it out. And I hope, Mr Chalmers, you'll do the same in the church.'

Margaret's face was red with embarrassment because the Rev. Frederick Chalmers was noted for his rather dry and dusty sermons and the *double entendre* had certainly not escaped his rapt attention.

The over-enthusiastic response to his factual commentary put Gibley off his final punch-line.

'And so I hope that this will be a successful sale. May I ask you to be very conservative in your giving—I mean liberal,' he corrected himself in his confusion, 'and I hope that your target will prove to be conservative and that your liberals, I mean labours, will be fully rewarded.'

Anxious to finish off quickly, he sat down muttering that he had much pleasure in declaring the Fête open.

The Rev. Chalmers had not been greatly impressed at the M.P.'s performance; the reference to 'dry rot' had wounded him deeply, but the courtesies of such occasions had to be followed.

'Thank you, Mr Horn, for your kind and encouraging words,' he announced in a louder voice to drown the noise resembling an Arab market-place which had broken out round the stalls when the word 'Open' had been said, 'and I will now call on Miss Patsy Goodall to make a presentation.'

At this point a pretty little girl dressed in white was pushed, protesting, on to the platform carrying an enormous bunch of flowers, which was clearly an unreasonable burden for one so young. She took a few faltering steps towards Margaret Horn who had risen in anticipation, then changed her mind and retreated towards the curtain once again.

A second push from the unseen hand prodded the child back on to the stage, whereupon Miss Patsy proceeded to collapse in a flood of tears. Ever responsive to feminine distress, Gibley stepped forward and patted her head, only to be rewarded with a spirited kick on the shin which, in turn, resulted in his letting loose an oath which was quite out of place in the West Church, especially before the ladies of the Women's Auxiliary.

After a few moments of confusion which amply confirmed the fact that Miss Patsy had no great regard for Mr Gibley Horn, the flowers were somehow or other transferred to the hands of Margaret and the party stumbled off the platform.

'Let me take you round the stalls,' said Mr Chalmers, with a certain lack of cordiality which had marked his initial welcome to the M.P. 'Mrs Hamilton can accompany your wife round separately.'

'I'll come round with you and Gibley,' said Margaret in a panic, realising that their joint fortunes were entirely in her husband's possession.

Any deviation from the carefully laid plans constituted a tedious irritation, and Mrs Hamilton was not happy at the information that she was a less acceptable guide than the Minister. But it was impossible to deny their guest's request and the four companions made for the Arts and Crafts Stall.

Drawing herself away from her other customers in anticipation of securing a major contribution to her stall, which had been the top performer in five successive Bazaars, Mrs Robertson gesticulated in Gibley's direction and, at the same time, displayed a grotesque great vase which had some figures painted round it by an amateurish hand.

'Can I interest you in this lovely flower vase which has been decorated by our own Miss Prichard? I'm sure that it would look beautiful in your home, Mr Horn. It's only priced at three pounds ten, but it would cost a fortune in the shops.'

This kind of pricey stuff didn't go well at bazaars; and Mr Horn was one of the few who might be persuaded to buy it.

'I don't think that I will take that,' said Gibley

without offering any comment on the object's artistic merit, lest Miss Prichard might be hovering near by.

Clearly showing her acute disappointment, Mrs Robertson was invited by Margaret to rummage round for a tea cosy. An appropriate object was soon discovered and Gibley paid the exact price which was 13/11d.

Their departure to the Groceries Stall left Mrs Robertson in a gloomy state of mind. If trade continued at its present depressed level, Mrs Milligan's Groceries Stall might bring in a larger total than Arts and Crafts. And if this tragedy occurred, it would be that idiotic M.P. who was to blame. To think that she had argued for a large bouquet for Mrs Horn in the Committee in the full knowledge that, immediately after receiving her handsome gift, the M.P.'s wife would be confronted with Arts and Crafts.

'Did you hear what that man said when he bumped into little Patsy on the platform?' she inquired of Miss Prichard as if to confirm the extent of Gibley's iniquity.

Poor Miss Prichard had not heard anything—she had been too nervously apprehensive about the management of her part of the stall to bother about what was happening up there. But she was awake enough to gather from her stall convener that the M.P. must have uttered a highly inappropriate sentiment, and she pondered this outrage in her heart.

After visiting all the stalls and creating the general impression that they must have mistaken the Bazaar for a Woolworth's Sale, the M.P. and his wife were privileged to enjoy the companionship of the Minister

and the Bazaar convener at afternoon tea; and, thereafter, they departed hurriedly clutching a parcel containing one tea cosy, one hairy pair of socks labelled
'gent' but clearly designed for an Eskimo, one caddy
of tea, two bottles of pickled something, a plastic
writing case and a substantial round fruit cake, which
could have substituted effectively for a curling stone
had it been decorated with a steel handle instead of a
white candle which bore a number of dirty finger-
prints.

But in addition to this treasure-trove, they also
departed with one shilling and fivepence in their
pockets which, at least, was cause for satisfaction.

On the way home, the car began to splutter just
beside a petrol station and, with a desperate effort,
Gibley made the journey to the pump marked '5/9 per
gallon — no credit'. But it was credit that Gibley was
seeking, as he doubted the ability of the pump attendant (who was clearly of a less-gifted intellectual
category) to work out how many 5/9s went into one
shilling and fivepence. It was only when he spoke by
telephone with the owner of the garage that credit
facilities over the week-end were arranged and he
charged Margaret with the responsibility of ensuring
that the Yellow Moon Garage would not regret the
trust which its owner had placed in the local M.P., by
delivering the cash on Monday.

'Shouldn't have been so difficult,' said Margaret.
'The garage owner is Mr Hamilton whose wife was the
Convener of the Sale. What did you tell him?'

'That I had spent a fortune at a Church Bazaar and

was cleaned out of ready cash,' said Gibley with a groan. And already he could imagine the chief topic of conversation at the next meeting of the West Church Women's Auxiliary. . . .

✳✳✳   ✳✳✳   ✳✳✳

'These Press reports made you look a bit of a chump,' Major Perkins advised Gibley confidentially after dinner was over and the ladies had withdrawn to the drawing-room.

Taking another glass of Gibley's port he made the further pregnant observation, 'Very tight constituency this. Mustn't let the people think we're putting up a chump for them to vote for.' Ever since his installation as Chairman, the Major had made it clear to Gibley how seriously he took his responsibilities to the Party for putting up a suitable candidate for a tight constituency.

Gibley hastened to acknowledge that, to the politically immature, he might indeed have appeared to be a 'chump', but he expected his loyal supporters to appreciate that the whole wretched business of the Rossford Chemicals exchange and also the Tayworth Buildings row had been evilly and inaccurately manufactured by the Press.

Major Perkins still wore the expression of one who considered that he was not being told the whole and absolute truth. He had never, he reminded himself, been entirely happy with Gibley Horn as the M.P. They were a reasonable bunch, in his view, the Rossford Conservatives. Didn't expect their M.P. to be always shouting his top off or hitting the headlines. But equally, they did not expect him to make a prize chump of himself and have all the papers writing about it. And that television show last night had been, to say the least of it, unimpressive. He did not claim to be an expert on all this power nonsense, but he had gained the clear impression from the programme that the Labour and Liberal representatives knew their stuff and that old Gibley had been without the proverbial clue.

'Saw the T.V. show last night,' he introduced the subject in an unargumentative way, but clearly hoping for an explanation of Gibley's cluelessness which would make sense to his colleagues in the Rossford Conservative Club.

'I had the pair of them gunning for me,' said Gibley defensively.

'Couldn't you have read up the stuff in books and papers?' Major Perkins was clearly not satisfied with this answer.

'Didn't have time. My plane from London was late. Terrible rush. That fellow Donnelly hurried me into the studio before I knew where I was. Always knew he was one of these bloody Socialists. Studio was crawling with these long-haired Amerbala agitators.'

'Well the boys in the Club weren't happy. Think you should have thumped the Labour chap a bit more.'

'If they had suffered the way I did yesterday, they would have been flat on their backs,' countered Gibley rather huffily.

It sprang immediately to Major Perkins's mind that

any of the Rossford Conservative Club members might, even in this horizontal state, have performed as effectively on television as this M.P. had done; but he was by nature a kindly man and he declined to say so.

Instead, he put forward a more constructive suggestion.

'What's the business in the House on Monday?'

'Pensions Amendment Bill. Unimportant, uncontroversial stuff. One-line Whip,' Gibley played down the significance of the Bill as he suspected that Major Perkins, in one of his thoughtful flashes, was about to suggest that the whole situation might be salvaged if the M.P. were to rush down on Monday and make a dramatic oration in the House of Commons, which would capture the headlines and restore the people's faith in the worth of their Parliamentary representative.

'Splendid,' responded the Major. 'We have an Association Executive Meeting on Monday night at eight p.m. You can come to that and, at least, make peace with your own supporters. It might avert some criticism.'

Major Perkins was well aware that the more troublesome members of the Executive would take the opportunity of commenting on Gibley's behaviour, and he did not fancy having to repeat the M.P.'s explanations to such a critical audience. Let the M.P. come and speak for himself.

'I'm afraid that I have a terribly important meeting in the House on Monday,' Gibley explained. 'Couldn't put it off now. Tell the Executive how sorry I am.'

Major Perkins looked a little put out at this.

'Who the blazes are you meeting?' he asked, hoping at least to have a respectable excuse to make for the M.P.'s absence.

Gibley just could not bring himself to advise his Chairman that the 'terribly important meeting' was with the office-bearers of the Insect Friendship League and so he said quietly, 'Forget it. I'll fly up for the meeting.'

'Good,' said the Major. It would be much more convincing to tell the Committee that the M.P. had flown up specially to see them, instead of making the usual short trip from 'Beechgrove' after a day's plunking from Parliament at home. He also felt gratified that a quiet word from him should have persuaded Horn to go four hundred miles out of his way.

'Always keep our man on his toes,' he invariably boasted at the Regional meetings to other Constituency Chairmen who still looked with disbelief at this man who could tell the Member of Parliament where to get off.

And he sank back farther into the armchair after taking another satisfying swig at the port.

***   ***   ***

On Sunday, Gibley and Margaret managed to get away in the car for a drive. They stopped at a lay-by in a minor road to have a breath of the clear country air punctuated with blasts of petrol fumes from time to time. Gibley was always at his most childish and emotional when worried. As he saw a delightful little hedgehog stumbling across the tarmac road his heart sang joyfully, as though in the humble and uneventful happenings of nature he could find rest and solace from the cruel and callous world. He remembered Harry the Hedgehog in that little brown book which he had once read to Keith, when he was a child. He could imagine that the prickly little chap was rushing away to a meal of acorn pancakes and dandelion tea which Rosie the Rabbit would have by now laid out on a fresh white tea-cloth under the oak tree.

'Zoom. Splat.' With a roar an open sports car driven by a fiendish-looking fellow with a red beard and navigated by an obnoxious-looking girl smoking a cigarette had suddenly roared past and, in place of Harry, there was only a twisted lump of blood and prickles lying on the road.

It's a dirty cruel world, thought Gibley as he switched on the ignition and pulled out fiercely on to the road.

✳✳✳   ✳✳✳   ✳✳✳

As he strode into the House of Commons on the Monday morning, Gibley was conscious of two problems which the day might bring. First he would have in his mail the reply to the questions which he had put down last week about BX20. If there was no joy from them, he might have to have a difficult interview with Miss Phillimore and advise her to seek another Galahad. Worse still, he would have to find another Bill in time for it to be presented by the following Tuesday.

If all was well, he could go ahead with his meeting at 4 p.m. with the League and try and pick their brains for the basis of a speech.

He walked in by the massive St Stephen's Entrance. One of the few consolations which he received these days from being an M.P. was that short, sharp and business-like march through the door which the policemen on duty would whip open smartly with a cordial 'Good morning, Mr Horn', while the spectators crowding round outside, and excluded from entering the building on a Monday morning by virtue of their humble position in Society, would look in awe at the sight of this great man striding confidently through the door to grapple with the problems of the nation.

Gibley always got a kick out of this little ceremony, and on this of all mornings he was looking for comfort.

'Support freedom in Amerbala,' shouted a knot of demonstrators, clearly assuming that one so immaculate in bearing and carriage would have some say in the destinies of the people of that wretched Coastal Strip.

Turning to look condescendingly at the peasants who had so addressed him, Gibley hurried in with the air of someone who had greater problems to overcome.

'Enthusiasts!' he joked with the policeman on duty who, mindful of the fact that public servants did not have opinions and playing for safety less this remark conveyed, however indirectly, approval or criticism for one of the policies of Her Majesty's Government, simply replied that it was a nice day.

Gibley tramped up the stairs past the historic West-minster Hall to St Stephen's Hall with its pictures of scenes from English history. (What a thrill this walk had given him the first few days, ten years ago!) And now he entered the great Central Lobby where crowds gathered to meet their M.P.s and convey opinions to them when the House was in session. 'Join the mass Lobby to save freedom and democracy in Amerbala,' he had read scrawled on a wall on his journey to the House. That meant that there would be a mass of these scruffy individuals pouring into the Lobby, some time this week, to surround their M.P.s and hurl slogans at them. How lucky he was to have a Constituency so far away that he was virtually untroubled by such activities.

Away to the right was the corridor to the House of Lords. What a splendid place that was! Still surviving despite all attempts to abolish it. You could spend your time there with no constituents to bother about and make a speech only when you wanted to. He would certainly have yearned for a peerage if the pay had been better. Mind you, it was easier to get if you had a cast-iron majority to surrender in exchange, but Ross-ford's meagre 3,000 was no gift, particularly when the Government was under such attack.

No House of Lords for you, Gibley. At least not today, he mused, and quickly turned his face away from Mecca and walked along to the Members' Lobby of the House of Commons. The place was deserted, apart from a few secretaries who had been to the Post Office for their masters' mail. He stepped smartly into the Post Office and immediately heard one of the men behind the counter shouting 'Gibley Horn' into a speaker fixed to the wall.

Within seconds there was a low rumble indicating the fact that a bundle of letters was tumbling down a chute.

Quite soon he was the proud recipient of a substantial bundle of letters all having in common his name typed, written or scrawled over the front of the envelope.

He hastened to the library and started to investigate the contents of this mass of correspondence.

'I wish to protest at your approval of the closure of the chemical factory at Manendon which has come as a shock to . . .' Someone had been quick off the mark. How could he put this one right? He tore open another envelope and read—

'I have always been a Conservative and have always voted for you and wonder if you can help me to get a house. The housing people know about my political views and I never get a chance. Change your politics, my neighbour says, and you'll get one, no bother. But not me. I live just now in a two-apartment flat in . . .' If all these people had voted for him, how had he managed to get only a 3,000 majority? Gibley thrust the letter on one side and selected from the pile one written on mauve notepaper—

'I am instructed by the Committee of the Current Affairs Section of the Rossford Townswomen's Guild to invite you to speak to the members on Friday, 9th September. I suggest for the subject . . .'

A quick look at his diary confirmed that this could

indeed be arranged. The T.G.s were a pleasant bunch and could be guaranteed to laugh heartily at his meagre store of Parliamentary witticisms. He glanced hurriedly through the remaining letters with fourpenny stamps.

'I am writing to seek your views on the present problem in Amerbala where British troops have been sent in. . . .' That was an easy one to answer. Could count on at least one satisfied customer. Oh, dear, dear! It was one of the other crowd. '. . . typical of the gunboat mentality which has been outdated by the march of freedom and democracy in the emergent nations.' He would have to be careful with this one. But no matter what he wrote, it wouldn't make any difference.

'I have had a long correspondence with you about my army pension which the Government have refused to pay and am again writing to demand that my case be raised in Parliament with the Prime Minister—Sir Oliver. . . .'

How many times had he told that fellow that the Board had decided that his limp had nothing to do with his two years' army service when he had fought to defend the nation's liberty in the kitchens of Aldershot? And how could he convince him that the Prime Minister did not answer questions about pensions? He would just have to try again.

There were also three replies from Ministers about matters on which he had written to them, in each case with an enclosed copy of the letter which could be sent on to the constituent concerned. He remembered reading that these letters cost the Civil Service over

£10 each and hoped that his constituents would be mindful of the time and trouble which their inquiries had necessitated.

He also had the usual batch of magazines, circulars and newspapers, but these made a speedy journey to the wastepaper basket, the more easily recognised ones even being deprived of the privilege of being taken out of their wrappings.

And then there were two buff envelopes marked 'Parliamentary Answers'. 'Immediate.' Gibley opened the first hesitantly, wondering what surprises were in store for him.

'Mr Gibley Horn (Rossford—Cons.),' he read, 'to ask the President of the Board of Trade what quantity of the chemical known as BX20 has been imported from the U.S.A. in each of the past five years and what was the cost in each year?'

Then there was the reply:

'Mr Ian Forbes Paton—I regret that I do not have the information which the Hon. Gentleman seeks, but I understand that imports have been in the order of £4m to £6m in each of the past three years. The figure for the current year should be lower in view of the fact that the chemical is now being manufactured under licence in Great Britain.'

Not a great deal of information. He would have to think about this. But now to the other one:

'Mr Gibley Horn (Rossford—Cons.) to ask the Minister of Agriculture what information he has regarding the extent to which chemical insecticides containing BX20 are used in Britain and in foreign countries, and what specific information he has regarding the position in the United States and in Paraguay.'

'Sir Albert Needholm—I am advised that chemical insecticides containing BX20 were introduced some six years ago and have been used by British farmers for around four years. An exact estimate cannot be made, but it is understood that approximately one third of the cornfields in the country have been treated with insecticides of the type mentioned.

'These chemical insecticides are now used extensively in Europe and South America, but I have no information about their use elsewhere. It is true that the insecticides were first used in Paraguay where they were successful in eliminating insects of the elyhonbrae variety, the nearest British equivalent being the Spotted Hummerfly.

'The insecticides are not used in North America.'

So these Insect League people were right! Not used at all in the U.S.A. Did they have information in the States showing the dangers, or were they merely experimenting with doubtful chemicals in other countries to see if the inhabitants were poisoned before they tried them out in their own country? This could be dynamite. He must have a chat with John Knox-Crichton about this.

As he climbed up the stairs to the Agency Office to dictate his correspondence, he felt excited by this vital information which he had discovered.

Having dealt with his mail, he came down to the Lobby again and there saw, to his delight, that John

Knox-Crichton was standing talking to one of the Labour Members.

'But I must get away on Thursday,' he was protesting. 'I used to cover up for you when your crowd was in power. The Whips were getting quite shirty about it.'

After further haggling, the reluctant Labour man agreed to 'pair' on the Thursday, which is the Parliamentary way of describing a system whereby Members belonging to either side both agree to stay away from votes at the same time. The pair then disengaged and Knox-Crichton was thus laid open to Gibley's enthusiastic approaches.

'Remember these Questions you said I should put down?'

'What Questions?' replied John Knox-Crichton, clearly needing some time to collect his thoughts which had been scattered round his head by the possibility of not getting a 'pair' for Thursday.

'The ones about BX20—you know my Bill for the Insect League,' Gibley conveyed the essential clues in the minimum of words.

'Oh, that crowd of loonies? Yes, I remember.'

John Knox-Crichton instinctively shrank at the mere mention of the Insect Friendship League with all its associations with his Aunt Emily, but he did remember Gibley mentioning that stuff which the Americans were dishing out to the people of Paraguay, in a typical Santa Claus gesture, while at the same time having nothing to do with the poisonous stuff themselves. This looked like a splendid story. Just the kind of thing on which he could ventilate his passionate dislike of the United States. (His conscious mind hastily rejected any suggestion that this dislike stemmed from that terrible holiday in Nice which had been ruined by the presence of an obnoxious Texan, but it was strange how he always thought of Elmer Pottinger Jnr. and his uncivilised conduct in the hotel dining-room whenever the word 'America' was mentioned.)

'Well, I got the replies,' cried Gibley excitedly. 'Look.' He thrust the papers into Knox-Crichton's hands.

'The insecticides are not used in North America.' My goodness! So there appeared to be something in this. Old Gibley had stirred up a hornet's nest after all.

'I've been thinking that I should get on to the American Embassy and ask them for their views and comments,' Gibley suggested.

'Do that and they'll have a statement all ready to squash the whole story within hours,' John stated authoritatively. 'They'll have the world convinced that the farmers in the States are making a noble sacrifice to help out the underprivileged people of Paraguay before you have a chance to let the story loose. Keep the whole thing under your hat just now.'

'I'm meeting the Executive Committee of the League at four o'clock,' Gibley announced. 'Would you like to come along, as one of the sponsors of my Bill?'

'Not likely,' his colleague respectfully indicated. 'That loonie Himmelstein and his mob of cranks! Not me!'

'It will be a short meeting,' Gibley pleaded. 'I have

to catch the six-fifteen plane to Glasgow; so I will have to be clear of them by about half past four.'

But words could not weaken the resolve of the Member who had already had the pleasure of meeting the Committee through the courtesy of Aunt Emily.

'Give them my apologies,' he suggested, 'and then run.'

This considerable progress cheered the Rossford M.P. a little, but his jollity quickly turned to gloom as some other Scottish M.P.s arrived in the House offering their cold comments on his week-end's work.

'Any more council houses collapsing?' said one Tory cheerfully, not appreciating just how sensitive his colleague was on the subject.

'Closed down any more factories?' questioned another.

Some, of course, quietly and sympathetically indicated that the whole business was sad, and what wretched chaps these Press men were. But Gibley had a well-founded suspicion that their assessment of the position would be very different in the presence of M.P.s other than himself. He knew that in a few hours, by the unique Parliamentary bush telegraph, the word would have got round that Gibley Horn had made an ass of himself. In these circumstances he did not look forward to joining his colleagues in the Dining Room and sped forthwith to the dungeons to have a self-service meal in the Cafeteria there.

After he had taken the advice of the management and purchased chicken soup (at least they thought it

was chicken soup, or it might be mushroom or vege-
table) and haddock and chips, he looked round the
tables and saw in a corner the hunched figure of Peter
McGarrity whom he had met last at Glasgow Central
Station the previous Sunday night.

'Can I join you, Pete?' he asked pleasantly.

Pete's affirmative grunt indicated that he would be
honoured.

'Rough time you've had with the Press,' Pete
volunteered.

Deeply appreciative of the honest response he could
always get from McGarrity, Gibley decided to test his
Scottish colleague further.

'How bad do you think it looks?'

'Terrible. And people don't forget that kind of stuff.
The important thing is not to fall out with the Press
boys over it. Be nice to them. Smile. And then they'll
eventually feel so guilty that they'll write you up big
on some human-interest story.'

This was good advice. Gibley could recognise it
immediately, as Pete was one of the shrewdest boys in
the business. He could also sum up any one of his 629
colleagues in a flash. He did not dislike Gibley,
although he recognised that he was a bit of a pompous
ass, and he did not like the way the Press had cut up
the Rossford M.P.

'Worst thing you can do is to write to the editors, or
criticise the reporters, or complain to the Press Council.
That will just antagonise them and they'll persecute
you for years. That's what happened to old Joe
Simpson.'

Gibley could not remember old Joe Simpson well, because he had been an ex-Member of the House before
Gibley joined it. But he did recall that the only references
to him in the papers had been adverse criticisms, and he
had consequently gained the impression that the said
Joe Simpson was both stupid and irresponsible.

'One of the nicest blokes on God's earth,' Pete corrected the impression immediately. 'But he fell out with
the Press over the way they reported a mine disaster
story. Forced one of them to print a retraction. Worst
thing possible. That was the end of old Joe. If he had
jumped into the canal to rescue an old-age pensioner
the papers would have said he did it just to pinch the
old fellow's watch and chain.'

'That's very good advice indeed,' said Gibley grate-
fully, 'but what should I say to the Press boys just now,
nothing? Or should I make a statement. My Chairman
thinks I should.'

'Shoot your Chairman,' said Pete. 'It's your hide,
not his. Just say to the Press boys that they had a fair
crack at you and smile a bit, but look wounded. Then
tell them that your wife was very upset. That'll make
the b's feel bad. Then go along to them next time you
have a good human-interest story and you'll be amazed
at the result. But don't get any ideas that the Press is
against you. They only do their job and you gave them
two wonderful stories.'

Pete returned to his soup and thereby signified that
the free consultation was over.

'Tell me about this Knox-Crichton fellow,' continued Pete, after a pause. 'You seem to go round with

him a lot.' Pete's careful assessment of Parliamentary trends and of the calibre of individual M.P.s was the result of studious and cunning tapping of every possible source of information. And he saw in Gibley's gratitude a good opportunity to get some dope about one Tory M.P. about whom he knew very little. He was not disappointed.

Gibley enjoyed his lunch with Pete who was, in his opinion, one of the real gentlemen of the House, and he was startled to hear the bell ringing to signify that half past two had struck and the Speaker was already at Prayers.

He made for the Library and decided to write some notes for his meeting that night with the Executive Committee of the Rossford Conservative Association.

But, as he sat down at one of the tables, he felt suddenly lazy. As he scribbled, he looked round hopefully for one of these interruptions that one could always count on in the Library despite the fact that it was amply covered with notices signifying the desirability of silence. He did not have long to wait.

Along came Paul Maxwell with a bundle of copies of what was clearly a Motion in his hands—hands which must have grown weary under the strain of patting the backs and shaking the hands of those who might be able to assist him on the road to advancement which was clearly his destiny. Maxwell was young, enthusiastic, ambitious and talkative. He was one of the new generation of proletarian Conservatives who seemed to be truly in touch with the people and knew their problems and aspirations with the intimacy which social survey computer programmes alone could bring. While he had never actually seen a stairhead closet, he could have told Gibley that 1,916 of the good people of Rossford laboured under the disadvantages which this plumbing arrangement could inflict. And while his whole being was repelled at the prospect of joining the less-gifted and ill-washed crowds which poured into football grounds on Saturdays, he knew that one in five male adults made a habit of attending a match at least once every five weeks. He couldn't write out an acceptable three-cross double for all the coffee in Brazil, but he was acutely aware that the average family spent 2/4½d per week backing their fancies at racecourses. This information was, of course, an essential feature of the social conscience of which he was the proud possessor, and the absence of which he so sincerely deplored in many of his more reactionary colleagues. His own background was impeccable. Twenty-three years of residence with middle-class parents, who sacrificed selflessly to ensure that their son was given all educational opportunities and sheltered from the social stresses which they had experienced. The dear couple had been delighted when Paul's social conscience had prompted him to organise a sale of work in their garden to raise five pounds to finance an adventure playground for the underprivileged children of Stepney, but they would have been horrified if he had cycled four miles down the road to play there with the Stepney children.

He had spent six years of celibate and healthy study within the monastic solitude of the local grammar

school and had then four years of equally selfless
endeavour at a Redbrick University, topping a brilliant
academic career with a thesis on Working Class
Organisation between 1821 and 1850.

Thereafter, he had devoted his energies further to
the people through his position as assistant statistician
in the Research and Development Section of one of
the great oil companies whose offices were pleasantly
situated in a garden suburb of a great city. Three years
later, he had become convinced that the Conservative
Party was suffering from lack of involvement with
ordinary people and their problems and had decided
that he had a special vocation to redress the balance.

Having arrived at the House of Commons with the
assistance of 28,000 executives and technicians resident
in one of the commuter suburbs, he had addressed
himself conscientiously to transfiguring his unques-
tioned concern for the people into sympathetic legislation, designed to alleviate their distresses.

He had moved an amendment to the Health Benefits
Bill to increase the Maternity Allowance. '26·7 per cent
of young mothers do not provide babies with the appropriate feeding stuffs and 5·4 per cent of young children,
aged five, suffer from bone deformities which stem
from inadequate diets between the age of six and nine
months,' he had informed the House.

But the forces of reaction in the Party were still
thwarting him at every turn.

'It's a well-known fact that some young mothers
decide to have another baby so that they can pay off
hire-purchase debts with the maternity allowance and

this amendment will bring another baby boom,' that reactionary, Col. Jackson, had scornfully commented. The old fool was quite out of touch. He even admitted that he hadn't read Jemima Blacklaw's article on the Hull Survey of Working Class Budgets. So what could he know about the problem?

But talent will out. And, after only one year in the House, Paul had been elected joint-secretary of the powerful Social Affairs Study Group and the Group's paper on 'School Meals—Some new suggestions on policy' had even attracted favourable comment from Sir Oliver when he had been addressing the Infant Teachers' Conference at Llandudno.

The time would come when Col. Jackson and his reactionary friends would find that their unscientific attitudes, which could not be backed by any statistical evidence, would become as irrelevant in the Conservative Party as they were themselves.

But, in the meantime, his task covered a more limited field. Dr Gormly had published a paper in the *Education Awake* supplement showing that workers in heavy industry suffered complex psychological disturbances which affected their work attitudes after absences, through sickness, of more than five weeks' duration. Paul knew that this Report would be causing excited comment in working-class homes throughout the length and breadth of the land, and he was determined that the Conservative Party should not appear, as it had so often in the past, to be blissfully unaware of such a remarkable advance in the march of social knowledge. He and his friends in the Social Studies

Group had met late last night and he had been charged with the task of drafting an Early Day Motion on the subject, which task had kept him at his desk until the small hours. He had chosen the wording most carefully to avoid criticism on unscientific assumptions, and he had rushed down to the copying machine in the morning to produce forty copies of the Motion so that his colleagues could seek signatures of support at the same time as he did so himself.

He had been alarmed to find a new Labour Member already at the machine and, for a moment, was terrified lest he and his friends should have been pipped at the post by a similar motion signed by Socialist Members. But a hurried look had disclosed that the Member was simply doing copies of a speech to be given at a Miners' Day Gala and it seemed to be about this Amerbala problem, with not a word about *Education Awake* and its exciting article.

'That this House notes with concern the conclusions of Dr Gormly's paper in *Education Awake* regarding the psychological disturbances suffered by workers in heavy industry after absences through sickness, of more than five weeks' duration and, while appreciating that firm conclusions must await the publication and assessment of statistical data, considers that the evidence is sufficiently significant to warrant the matter being considered urgently by the Survey Section of the Ministry of Social Security.'

And there at the top of the Motion was his own name —Paul Maxwell—as the principal sponsor. If they could get a lot of names and hand in the Motion to the

Table Office tonight, it would be published in to-morrow's Order Paper before the Labour boys had wind of it. The Socialists would never get over this. And the Unions would see which Party really cared about the workers.

And in Gibley Horn he saw a possible supporter for this historic motion. He was actually quite fond of Mr Horn. He did not, for a start, regard him with the basic hostility with which he viewed all potential con-tenders for Office, as Gibley was clearly out of the race, if he had ever been in it. He also appreciated the fact that the old chap had signed two of his previous motions and had not treated them with the suspicion which other senior colleagues had demonstrated through reported comments like 'intellectual wet' and 'crawling little toad'. And the fact that he had pro-posed a system of tokens for fuel supplies to old age pensioners, while being a scheme which would not attract any favourable comment in any of the Uni-versity Social Departments, had at least shown that his heart was in the right place.

'Would you care to consider supporting a Motion which some of my colleagues have drafted, Mr Horn?' he asked politely.

'Certainly,' replied Gibley, and took out his pen as though to add his name to the document forthwith. He instinctively liked this new young chap. Very respect-ful, well educated. Reminded him of his son, Keith. And these motions which he took so seriously were harmless enough. They never said anything—at least, nothing he could understand. And even if they had said anything, it wouldn't matter, because the Motions simply appeared on the Order Paper and were never discussed or debated. The most that could be hoped for was a mention in the quality morning papers. And he could always send on a copy of the Order Paper to the *Rossford Gazette*. When short of copy, they sometimes put in a paragraph conveying the tidings that Mr Horn was sponsoring a Motion on housing, unemployment benefit or old age pensions. He was sure that the readers understood as little about the Motions as he did, but it gave the impression that he was doing something for O.A.P.s and other unfortunates. Yes, he would certainly sign this motion.

But, as he started to unclip his pen, Paul Maxwell looked a little startled and said:

'Aren't you going to read it first?' Paul would have liked, ideally, to think that Members signed his Motions only after deep thought and consideration. The prospect of someone signing, so freely, a Motion, the wording of which had caused him two hours of tortured soul-searching, was an affront to his intellect.

'Of course, of course,' said Gibley, and looked very serious all of a sudden. He took the paper from Paul and appeared to reflect deeply while he scanned the text.

'Yes, I'll support this gladly. Splendid stuff!'

He signed. Paul moved off, pleased that he now had the support of forty-one Conservative M.P.s who were deeply concerned at the implications of Dr Gormly's paper. But his pleasure disappeared suddenly when he observed the untidy and bear-like figure of Terry

Lester, his greatest foe, storming through the library in his direction with the racing section of the *Star* ostentatiously displayed under his arm.

Paul just could not understand Terry Lester. The papers said that he had come up the hard way and had been employed spasmodically as a circus-hand, coalheaver and brick-layer before the electors of Goolwich had returned him in a surprise election as their first Tory M.P. It seemed incomprehensible to Paul that someone with his roots so firmly entrenched in the working class should pour such scorn on his efforts, which were so selflessly directed towards improving the welfare of the underprivileged sections of society.

When he had suggested, discreetly, at the Commonwealth Affairs Committee that the dispute in Amerbala might be divested of its most inflammable aspects if a deputation of prominent Amerbala trade union leaders, who were organising a strike throughout the Coastal Strip, were invited to a round-table conference with British union chiefs, university lecturers and forward-looking Members of Parliament of both parties, Terry had interrupted with the comment 'Lock the hooligans up', an alternative proposal which had attracted an alarming amount of support. And when Paul had moved his amendment on increased maternity benefits in the House, he had been shocked to hear Terry interrupting from behind him with the coarse suggestion that if they increased the allowance any more, the Irish would be paying surtax.

He had constantly to console himself with the thought that Terry was by no means representative of the mass of the British people and that few, if any, of the 68·9 per cent of British families with incomes under £25 per week approached the great issues of the day with the ignorant unreasonable prejudice which Terry Lester demonstrated. Anyway, he would only be a flash in the pan, because Goolwich was basically a Labour seat and the electors there would no doubt return to their traditional loyalties by the next election. And to think that they had put out George Hindley-Highgate, who had written such erudite articles for the *University Social Review*, for this ruffian who was sheltering under the label of the Conservative Party! Paul wondered what the right-thinking people of Goolwich would think of the Conservatives. He must remember to speak to the Chairman of the Party about the need to put in an educated candidate there with progressive views, after Lester had been thrown out, as he surely would be.

'Morning, Professor,' cried Terry with characteristic disrespect when he saw the studious figure of his colleague. 'What's all this tripe you've been saying about grants for splitting up houses? Read it in the *Star* on Wednesday. All the grasping landlords in Goolwich are rubbing their hands. A Government subsidy to carve up old houses and let off the rooms at three pounds per week. Mad idea!'

How irresponsible can you get, thought Paul.

'I don't suppose you read the Report of the Wheeler Commission which showed that there were enough rooms in British houses to provide 2·9 rooms for every family?' he inquired huffily. 'If we converted all the

big underoccupied houses and provided an incentive to
do this, we could largely solve our housing problem.
The statistics prove it.'

'That Report's bunk,' boomed Terry. 'Can't see us
converting Buckingham Palace into spinsters' flats. Or
Chequers into council houses.'

Paul was, honestly, not aware whether Professor
Wheeler had included such dwellings in his survey or
not, but he readily appreciated that he would be
unable to convince his colleague. Anyway, he had
much more important things to do.

'Did you listen to the whole of my speech?' he asked
haughtily, knowing full well that nobody, even of
Terry's limited intellect, could possibly have listened
to all his arguments and still remain unconvinced.

'Sorry, Professor. Must admit I didn't. It was a one-
line whip till ten and there was a splendid wrestling
match at Clapham—Bruiser Beattie and Hank the
Hunk. Great stuff! Bruiser got a dislocated arm.
Thrown clean out of the ring.'

There was nothing more to be said and Paul strode
off feeling that his low opinion of his colleague had
been amply proved out of his own mouth.

'Hallo, Gibley old chap,' Terry hailed in a voice
which produced a huge grin on the face of the Rossford
M.P. 'Any tips for the three-thirty? Or are you too
busy carrying on with that blonde of yours?'

'That blonde' was the highly respectable wife of the
Guatemalan Minister of Overseas Affairs. When Gibley
had been exchanging polite compliments with her at a
tea-party in the House, Terry Lester had immediately

advised his colleagues that this was the seed of an illicit relationship. The suggestion had been the basis of many a ribald comment in the smoking-room and Gibley entered into the spirit of it with his usual good nature.

'Won't be seeing her till the week-end in Brighton,' Gibley advised with mock sorrow.

'Well, give her my love,' Terry exhorted, 'and tell her that I'm free next week-end.'

Gibley was always delighted to have a chat with Terry Lester. Nobody could help but admire a chap who could win a safe Labour seat, and Gibley remembered with pleasure the trip which he had paid to Goolwich to take part in a Brains' Trust in front of the members of the Goolwich Conservative Association. What a wonderful bunch they had been! Plenty of fun and enthusiasm. Thought the world of Terry! And what a completely different cup of tea from his own Executive Committee which, he reminded himself, he would be addressing that very night.

But the interruptions had taken up some time. It was now almost 3.45 p.m. Better go and look out for the deputation from the Insect League who would be arriving around 4 p.m.

He wandered through to the Members' Lobby and, as he passed through, saw the figure of the *Star* Lobby correspondent who made it clear, by his sudden movement to the door, that he had no great wish to meet the M.P. whom he had pilloried so devastatingly in Saturday's edition.

But, remembering the good advice which he had

been given, Gibley marched up to him with a smile and said, much to the Lobby man's astonishment:

'How are things with you, Bill? You fairly took a run at me on Saturday, but I suppose that I asked for it. You really put me in the soup in the Constituency, but I've got a hard skin. Mind you,' he whispered confidentially, 'my wife was most upset about it. Actually in tears on Saturday morning. But she'll get over it, poor girl. That's the worst of being married to an idiot like me.'

Bill was really astounded, because when he had seen the Rossford M.P. striding towards him he had assumed that he was going to offer a series of uncomplimentary remarks about the *Star*, its contents and the loutish rogues who wrote for it. And he would have understood this fine when he thought of the vitriolic copy which he had sent up North. 'This will finish old Horn,' he had thought. But here was the much sinned-against M.P. actually being friendly. Shame about his wife! He realised what Hell these girls must go through as wives of M.P.s.

'Well, I must admit that the story did look a bit rough in the paper,' Bill explained. 'But you know what editors are like. Always looking for sensational stories. And they actually chopped up my copy a bit.' This was true, in the sense that commas and exclamation marks had been added by the sub-editors, but Bill hoped that this statement would persuade Gibley that the dirty cracks and cruel comments were the work of a group of horrible men hidden within the walls of the newspaper office and not the product of the diseased mind of a Lobby correspondent.

'I don't blame them. Got to sell the papers and I set it up for them,' Gibley courteously suggested.

As the Rossford M.P. shuffled away towards the Central Lobby he left Bill Banks feeling very guilty indeed and firmly resolved to send up a nice friendly story about Gibley Horn.

And now for that Professor Himmelstein and his friends. . . .

✳✳✳   ✳✳✳   ✳✳✳

As he came into the Central Lobby, Gibley looked round the assembled throng to see if there was anyone there looking remotely like a Professor. But he drew a blank. There was certainly no lack of volunteers because several of the bystanders looked at Gibley very carefully indeed to see if they saw in his plump face and bald, shiny head the profile which had occupied the front of the Election Address which had been pushed through their letter-box last year. They were, every one, on the lookout for their own Member of Parliament and were hoping at the very least for a ticket for the Visitors' Gallery and, possibly, tea and cakes on the Terrace where they could identify the Parliamentary 'greats' and collect reminiscences to pass on to the folk back home. Extending their arms in reverse inaccuracy to when describing the length of the fish they had caught, they would say, 'You know, I was only that length away from Tubby Lucas; you know, that chap who's always on the telly and says "stuff and bunkum" when he gets annoyed.'

Some of them today, regrettably, would wait in vain for their Members because it was Monday and many of the inhabitants of the building had decided that the consideration of the Pensions Amendment Bill could proceed just as effectively without their personal participation.

It was always tricky to get tickets for visitors. If they bounced in about five o'clock it was pretty easy to get them into the Gallery, because the big speakers would have finished by then and only a handful of Members would be in the House. But if they appeared enthusiastically at two o'clock, wishing to get in for Question Time, it was wellnigh impossible. And it was by no means easy to explain to them why they could not get in when the lady down the street had been so privileged or when their cousin from Aberdeen had not only seen the Prime Minister in action, but had also had a delightful meal with her M.P. in the Dining Room. There was no doubt about the truth of this latter contention because the cousin frequently displayed the tea-spoon with the House of Commons crest which she had filched when, she hoped, her host had not been looking.

How lucky he was, Gibley thought, to have a distant constituency! London Members had a terrible time with visitors almost every day, and those wretched school parties to show round in the morning.

It had been thought that the opening of the big closed-circuit Television Hall would provide accommodation for all those who wanted to see the House in session, but the numbers visiting had increased dramatically ever since the proceedings had been televised and, in any event, those refused admittance to the Chamber itself and sent to the Closed Circuit Room felt that they were getting no more than they had already got in their homes. In fact it was *less* satisfactory because the daily Television Summary only showed the highlights and gave the impression that the House was in perpetual uproar and excitement, whereas the closed circuit invariably showed a handful of dreary men talking in an extremely boring fashion about some insignificant problem to a House that was virtually deserted.

The only problem for Gibley was in June and July when the Scottish folk, passing through London on the way to Continental holidays, took the opportunity to visit the House of Commons, and the local M.P.s had to run a virtual shuttle service to and from the Terrace and advance their prospect of 'coronaries' significantly by consuming four afternoon teas.

However, it would be some time before all that started again and the immediate problem was to locate the Professor. Three-fifty-five p.m.! Thought they would have been the types to be here an hour early. But not a sign.

Just to make sure that appearances were not deceptive, he asked the policeman to shout out the name through the Hall, and felt quite an idiot when the bystanders looked round to see who was anxious to make the acquaintance of Professor Agrario Himmelstein. The policeman seemed to enjoy shouting out that absurd name. But his linguistic efforts were not rewarded with the success they deserved. No Professor came forward.

At that point the telephone on the desk rang, and from the snippets of conversation he overheard, Gibley gleaned that the Professor and his party had indeed arrived at the front door of the St Stephen's Entrance. But, through one of these strange twists of fate which distinguish human life from mechanical existence, the party's arrival had coincided with the efforts of Constable Proctor to remove a tiresome wasp from his uniform and to bring the insect's miserable life to a speedy and humane end under his size 10, regulation boot. This activity had produced an angry reaction from one of the ladies in the party which had been followed up with a minor physical assault carried out with the assistance of an umbrella, and Constable Proctor was clearly reluctant to allow such violent people access to the building unless, as they claimed, Mr Gibley Horn, M.P. was waiting for them within and could vouch for their good behaviour.

Satisfactory assurances having been communicated by Mr Horn through the internal telephone, the party advanced up St Stephen's Hall towards the Lobby where Gibley had placed himself in a receiving position.

'So this is indeed the great Mr Gibley Horn!' exclaimed the bearded old gentleman at the head of the party. His voice bore a trace of an East European accent and he wore a long heavy coat which seemed more appropriate to the Siberian wastes than to London on a sunny afternoon.

Agreeably surprised by this greeting, Gibley hastened to confirm that they were viewing that great man in person and accepted, regally, the Professor's invitation to be introduced to his colleagues.

'Mr McGeorge Pratt, Vice-President of the League and Managing Director of Pure Food Supplies Ltd.' Mr McGeorge Pratt extended a limp hand which had just removed an offending drip from his small pointed nose.

'Mr Elphinstone Bradley, Treasurer and Editor of *Nature and Health Weekly*.' Gibley had always considered that magazines with such titles were designed to display portraits of musclemen and shapely women with the minimum of wearing apparel, but Mr Bradley's dull, languid and hopeless expression made it clear that he could not have experienced the excitement of seeing any such portraits for a long time. Probably one of these nuts and honey magazines.

'Miss Euphie Hunt. Social Convener.' Miss Hunt's agitated expression allied to her frail and tiny person seemed to indicate that the social activities of the League would not cause the local Watch Committee any great concern.

'And our good friend Miss Phillimore—Secretary.' Miss Phillimore was wreathed with smiles of recognition as though to convey to her colleagues that her intimate association with the M.P. was of long standing.

'I'm pleased to meet you,' Gibley said politely, but was prevented from making any further observation by the Professor's assurance that the honour was entirely that of the Executive Committee of the League.

'Do come right through to the Commons and we'll

go down to the Interview Room I've booked for you. I'm afraid that I have to catch a plane at six-fifteen p.m., so I can only stay for about half an hour.'

This was satisfactory and the party proceeded along the passage to the Members' Lobby and then down by the lift to Interview Room 'S' which was reserved for one hour in the name of Mr Gibley Horn.

When he arrived down there, he saw that several of his colleagues were just leaving the room. Included in the crowd were Iain Constable and his colleague, Rufus Harkins. But, from the stony glances and angry exchanges displayed by the M.P.s, Gibley gained the impression that all was not well in the Amerbala Action group. He heard the name of Romsey-Wheeler being mentioned and also the words 'sold down the river'. Could Romsey-Wheeler have broken out of the pressure group? If he had, thought Gibley, he's got more sense than I thought. Wonder what could have made him do that?

The downstairs Interview Rooms were traditionally the gathering place of the unofficial pressure groups; while the upstairs Committee ones were generally occupied by the official policy committees of the two parties. The Conservative policy groups had continued to exist in identical form after they had regained power and there was a group, or committee for every subject. Unlike other committees, M.P.s were not elected to join. Every Conservative M.P. was automatically a member of each committee in the sense that he could attend any meeting he chose.

But the M.P.s normally limited their attendance to

subjects in which they had a special interest. If, of course, some great issues arose, a committee meeting which normally attracted twenty M.P.s might suddenly find over a hundred attending. Gibley was not terribly interested in these committees, but he did make a point of going to the Scottish Members' Meetings every week and also, on occasions, to the Commonwealth Affairs and to the Social Services Committees. He attended the Commonwealth one, because he hoped that something would come out of this new English Speaking Nations and Commonwealth Free Trade Area idea. Much better in his view than getting mixed up with the European mob. And he went to the Social Services Committee because Sir Andrew Mellin had confidentially advised him, some time ago, that these funny left-wing boys attended the Committee in great numbers and were putting across some silly ideas which would have made Disraeli turn in his grave, and that it would help if some of the wiser and more mature members were to put in an appearance at the meetings.

Gibley was subsequently surprised to see that the 'left-wingers' seemed to be led by that nice young fellow, Paul Maxwell, and the whole thing was a little confusing. But he kept faith with Sir Andrew by going along as often as he could and rumbling a 'Hear, Hear' whenever the old chap spoke. Mind you, they talked a lot of drivel at the meeting. The only cheering aspect consisted of frequent spirited obscenities which came from the mouth of Terry Lester, usually when Maxwell was speaking and always to the considerable embarrassment of the lady chairman. 'Parliamentary language only, Mr Lester,' she would plead in desperation. 'No,' she would hasten to assure the Goolwich M.P., 'bugger is *not* a Parliamentary expression.'

Within each Party there were groups of disgruntled men and women and also little clusters of folk who believed that their Parties were not sticking rigidly to the narrow paths of ideological virtue. The Amerbala Pressure Group was one such body and they frequently had a discussion together before they made a row in the House itself or at the main Commonwealth Party Group. The pressure groups downstairs had no fixed membership and no fixed mandate, but the same people always seemed to be involved. In the old days it was the so-called 'right-wingers' who had disturbed the happy family spirit of the Tory Party: but ever since Sir Oliver had twisted the ideological compass a slight turn to the right and had gone so far as to indicate that 'While Her Majesty's Government fully support and uphold the Charter and objects of the United Nations, we cannot permit the organisation to usurp the constitutional functions of the British Nation in Amerbala', the threat to harmony had come from the other end of the political spectrum in the confederation commonly known as the Conservative Party. And although the appointment of Antony Appelton to a junior post in the Communications Ministry had not given this darling of the right much scope to exercise his ideological objectives, Sir Oliver had thus made it clear that the 'progressive' honeymoon was in eclipse.

The downstairs rooms were, of course, used also for meeting deputations and Gibley Horn was reasonably confident that the sight of him entering a room with his four companions would not spark off any rumours that he was instigating a major Party revolt.

'Is this where the Cabinet meets?' asked the politically illiterate Miss Euphie Hunt, and she seemed visibly distressed to learn that this was not the case.

'I hope that this isn't some secret document I'm not meant to see,' said Elphinstone Bradley, handing over to Gibley an Order Paper covered with doodles which had obviously been the work of Iain Constable or one of his friends.

'Not at all,' Gibley assured him. 'You can keep it if you like.' He thought for a minute that it would be a most agreeable sport to take the doodles along to a psychiatrist for assessment. 'A power-hungry maniac' would no doubt be the professional diagnosis.

'Let's get down to business,' said Gibley. 'Miss Phillimore came to see me about this Bill which the League was hoping to sponsor and I must say that I was most impressed by her arguments.'

Miss Phillimore was thrilled to hear this unsolicited testimonial and knew that Gibley had given her splendid ammunition in his statement to ward off any more attacks from Miss Hunt on the 'outrageous expenditure on pencils and rubbers in the League's office'. The next time the old crow had something to say, she would be reminded that these were the tools by which work could be done to influence Members of Parliament and achieve the League's objects through legislation. No point in being penny wise and pound foolish when the continued survival of the insect world was at stake.

'As a Member of Parliament, my interest is more in the effect of chemical insecticides on the food which humans consume, but Miss Phillimore showed me clearly that the objects of the League could effectively coincide with my own desires.'

One up again for Phillimore!

'I may say that I was particularly interested to know that the chemical BX20 was being extensively used in some South American states and in Great Britain with apparent harmful effects, at least in Paraguay, but not used at all in the United States itself. I put down some Parliamentary questions on this matter and you will see, from the *Hansard* which I have here, the replies which I received.' At this point he passed round Friday's *Hansard* to an audience which was clearly impressed that their endeavours were now in permanent record in so vital a document as the Official Report of the House of Commons.

This must certainly be reprinted in the League's monthly news sheet, thought Miss Phillimore. As well as the exciting news about the Bill. Her contributors had been disappointed so often. But now it seemed that the League was really 'going places'. No more worries about an extra fifteen shillings for pencils and rubbers. The I.F.L. would be Big Time.

'You will see that the answers seem to confirm what you claim, but we will need a lot more specific information,' Gibley continued. 'I had in mind to ask the American Embassy for their comments, but I'm warned that they would rush out a statement, in a few hours, explaining that the American farmers were simply depriving themselves of good healthy insecticides to help the underprivileged farmers of South America. They're a crafty lot,' he added, with the air of one taking his audience into his confidence.

The League's office-bearers were more than convinced by this reasoning and felt considerably heartened by the fact that they had entrusted their destinies to such a shrewd and far-seeing political figure as Mr Horn.

Gibley sensed their approval and continued somewhat pompously:

'But I would like to have all the information you have about the diseases which have appeared in Paraguay and other South American Republics as well as any proof that you can substantiate to link up the chemical and the disease. I will also need a lot of information and statistics to help me to check up some of the points I hope to make in my speech introducing the Bill.' What Gibley meant was that he wanted them to write his speech for him, but he could not very well put it as bluntly as that.

'Admirably put, Mr Horn. I am delighted that you, of all the Members of Parliament, have taken on our noble struggle,' the Professor spoke with emotion.

'I can promise you that all the resources, the very considerable resources of the Insect Friendship League, will be placed at your disposal, and although our thanks will be inadequate reward for your endeavours, you will have the undying satisfaction of knowing that millions of our friends in the insect world can look to the future with more confidence.' Mr Elphinstone

Bradley thought that this was an appropriate moment to clap his hands vigorously and he proceeded to do so. Miss Euphie Hunt looked as though she was going to cry. But Gibley Horn was sure that he had listened to enough of this cackle and was anxious to get some cold hard facts to back up the case which he by now believed, despite the League's oddity, was a good one.

'But I haven't got the Bill through yet, I've only got three supporters so far—one from each Party—and I'll need a lot more information to persuade the 628 other M.P.s,' Gibley blurted out, in the hope of bringing the League's exuberant office-bearers down to earth.

'And I'm sure that Mr Knox-Crichton was one of the three good men,' Miss Phillimore chipped in.

'Yes, he was,' Gibley confirmed to the lady's delight, but tastefully omitted to add that John Knox-Crichton was of the opinion that she and her friends were a pack of loonies.

'But this *information*,' he cried in desperation. 'I must have it, I haven't got much time to spare.'

The Professor was ahead of his colleagues in realising that some cold hard facts must be forthcoming, if a beautiful friendship was not to evaporate.

'The file, Miss Phillimore, please,' he announced gravely as though he was about to produce for the Rossford M.P. the stone tablets specially brought down from Mount Sinai.

Miss Phillimore rummaged in her brief-case and handed the Professor a large yellow file which was clearly marked 'BX20' at the top and 'Confidential' in bold red letters at the foot as if to impress upon the

James Bonds of this world that such matters were not for their eyes.

Adjusting his spectacles to make quite sure that they were still fixed to his wizened face, the Professor proceeded to extract some press cuttings from the file and passed them over to the M.P.

'*Daily Star*, February 12th,' he read. 'Reports came in from Paraguay over the week-end about outbreaks of a strange disease which appeared to affect the stability of several hundred inhabitants of the rich corn-growing central belt. Local doctors claim that the disease, known as "falling fever", was first noted last year but that the numbers affected recently have grown alarmingly. A team of medical experts has been rushed to the area from the United States as a result of prompt State Department intervention, but they admit to being puzzled by the outbreak. People chiefly affected are agricultural workers in the corn fields and, so far, the population of the industrial centres is unaffected. People suffering from "falling fever" become aware of the malady only when they suddenly discover that they cannot walk or stand without falling over.'

That seemed to be pretty conclusive proof but still the Rossford M.P. was not satisfied. Circumstantial evidence—true enough—but he had to persuade hard-headed M.P.s. Knowing what he did, he was not surprised to find that the disease only occurred in the corn-growing areas nor did it astonish him that American doctors had been rushed to the area with such unusual haste. But he would like some more authoritative proof.

'And have there been any more outbreaks of the disease?' he asked suspiciously.

'Look at this,' the Professor stated triumphantly.

Again the *Star* was the source of information.

'Agricultural workers in Yorkshire were reported at the week-end to be suffering from a strange illness, the symptoms of which were a mystery to local doctors. The men find difficulty in standing or walking without falling over and those affected, about twenty in number, have been removed to the local hospital. Joseph Muldoon (29), a farm labourer, sustained injuries to his arm and leg when he fell into a water trough while suffering from the disease. His wife Florrie, attractive mother of three, commented, "I'm not surprised. With all the chemical stuff the lads have to work with these days, they can't help getting strange illnesses. I'm seeing my lawyer about compensation."

'Footnote:—There were reports last month of agricultural workers in Paraguay suffering from a similar disease, but a spokesman of the Health Ministry said that he had no evidence to link the outbreaks.'

Well! Well! This was quite alarming. If nothing was done, Gibley could see people in every part of the world staggering around and falling into water troughs.

'Have you any more information which could help me?' he asked.

'My Presidential Address,' replied the Professor, as if to indicate that, of all the possible authoritative documents, this was certainly the most significant. 'Then we have some more Press cuttings. There is also a letter from an American scientist who has our cause at heart.'

This might be interesting, thought Gibley.

'My dear Professor,' the letter began, 'While so many of my colleagues in the world of science are polluting the good earth with their fiendish potions, I joy to hear that the learned men of England are joining in the noble struggle. . . .'

Looked like a nut-case, unfortunately. All depends on his qualifications. That meant a lot in the Commons. If a statement was not read from the quality papers, or quoted from a man with at least ten letters after his name, nobody would pay much attention to it. But the only letters which this chap had after his name were F.I.P.F., and when Gibley learned that this signified that the Institute of Pure Food (Wisconsin) had made him an Honorary Fellow he dismissed this letter from his consideration.

'Is this all you have?' he asked.

'We have much more in the office. Only the vital materials have been brought with us. Primarily we came here to meet our distinguished sponsor and see with our own eyes the man who had been entrusted with our noble mission. This we have done.' The Professor's voice boomed—'My fellow office-bearers are as proud and delighted as I am to have made your acquaintance.

'We must rectify the balance of nature which has been so cruelly upset by the Quislings of science. We must safeguard the creatures of this world entrusted to our care. And, most of all, we must remember our friends of the insect world who for years, indeed for generations, have been without a champion. And now we have the champion in your good person, Sir. We wish you the success which your noble cause merits.'

Having delivered this oration, again to applause from Mr Bradley, the Professor stood up and shook the hand of the Rossford M.P. as though Gibley were about to set off for the jungle to rescue the Queen of Sheba, and the rest of the deputation rose to leave.

After escorting the party from the precincts, Gibley could not quite make up his mind whether the meeting had been a success. He had collected that interesting information about 'falling fever'. He had obtained promises of more information about Spotted Hummer-flies and the effects of insecticides. But there was still no 100 per cent proof. He had, however, been impressed by the respectful reverence which the deputation had demonstrated and their grateful appreciation of his efforts. After the battering around he had experienced recently, this had come as welcome relief. He was sure that Professor Himmelstein had never heard of the Tayworth Buildings 'scandal' or about his factory closure gaffe, and he was sure that even if the gentleman had been advised of these two events he would certainly not have believed them.

But now he had to depart again for Glasgow. And the shortage of time would mean another expensive taxi ride to London Airport—so there goes that 'saving like mad' promise again, he reflected sadly. He would have to keep these £4 journeys in mind and see if the tax man would allow them.

Again, he was blessed with a talkative taxi-driver but, being in a reasonably good humour, Gibley was prepared to converse. The taxi-driver, after discovering by devious means that his customer was a Conservative (he had suspected this all the time because not many Labour ones had bowler hats and umbrellas), proceeded to wax eloquent on the sins of the Socialist Party.

'Never get my vote again!' he exclaimed. Years of experience had taught him that his M.P. clients much preferred the reformed rake and the prodigal son to the constant believer. It always cheered them to discover, when returning to their constituencies, that one humble soul had seen the light, as it led them to conclude that taxi-drivers and others among their own voters would be arriving at the self-same conclusions.

A good-humoured client inevitably proved to be a generous one, and Jake Jennings was just the chap to instil his virtue in the taxi-travelling public.

Jake smiled to himself when he thought of all the Tory, Labour and Liberal M.P.s who must have told meetings and committees about his political conversion. 'The tide is turning,' he could almost hear them say. 'Why, only last night, the taxi-driver taking me to the airport said that he would never vote for the other Party again.' There were no limits to his versatility. Why, even last week, he had confidentially assured a certain burly chap that, if he lived in Scotland, his support would certainly go to the Scottish Nationalists. And the 5/- tip which had eventually emerged had almost convinced him that he would.

And here was another ripe plum for the picking.

'The way I see it, sir,' he suggested tentatively, 'the

Conservatives are the ones with the business experience. Running a country's a big business and you need folk with a good education to do it. Take this Amerbala business,' he referred to the specific example which had solidified his sentiments, 'Labour are making idiots of themselves. Bet you, few of them ever saw a shot fired in anger!'

With the exchange of such splendid sentiments the journey proceeded and, when the driver announced that the fare was £3 12s 6d, Gibley had no hesitation in departing without taking any change from the four pound notes which he proffered in payment.

Unencumbered by any luggage this time, Gibley stepped forward to check in with a little more confidence than usual, but he was still apprehensive about the journey by plane. Wretched things, planes! If they hadn't invented them, Major Perkins couldn't have expected him to come to the meeting tonight. And he realised, all of a sudden, that while a whole series of interesting events had filled his life since the dreadful events of last Friday, the newspapers of Saturday and the television performance of Friday would still be very fresh in the minds of his Executive Committee.

What a terrible crowd they were! Always narking about something when they weren't pulling each other's hair out. Always resigning and then returning under protest. He remembered the embarrassing visit he had been forced to pay to Mrs Cole-Pratt, the Ladies' Convener, to persuade her to withdraw the resignation which she had immediately submitted when Alec Anderson, then recently appointed as agent,

had asked Mrs Burns to give the vote of thanks to Lady
Mary Fox-White after she opened the Annual Fête.

'I've always given the vote of thanks and there's
never once been a complaint. But if you think you can
manage better without me, just go ahead. I've had
more than enough.'

Poor Gibley had been forced to listen for three-
quarters of an hour to the decimation of the said Mrs
Burns by major verbal surgery on the part of Mrs
Cole-Pratt, before a solution had eventually been
arrived at.

'Just in the Association three years and only living in
Rossford for five years in one of these new scheme
houses,' Mrs Cole-Pratt had announced with distaste,
'and that stupid new agent asks *her* to give the vote of
thanks at the Fête. When I think of all I've done for
the Conservative Party. Mr Oswald would *never* have
allowed it,' she referred in sympathetic terms to the
late departed M.P. with the obvious implication that,
if Gibley Horn was worth his salt, he would do likewise.

The compromise arrived at was that Mrs Cole-Pratt
would have afternoon tea with Lady Mary Fox-White
and that Mrs Burns would be totally and completely
banished from the tea-room while this jolly party was
in session. The whole scheme had nearly broken down
when Lady Mary had announced that she did not feel
like tea that afternoon, and it had needed the combined
efforts of the official party of five to convince her, in
desperation, that afternoon tea was just what she
needed and that there never had been such cream
cakes as were available that day.

But the whole sad episode had left a deep wound, and it was questionable whether the two ladies would ever have anything in common, apart from a deep and lasting hostility to each other.

Then there were the Young Conservatives. Always having barbecues and car rallies and getting married to each other or joining the Liberals when their romances went through a stony patch. And they were always sending him idiotic policy resolutions and expecting him to stand up in the House of Commons and tell the Prime Minister that the Rossford Young Conservatives and all right-thinking people considered that he was off his chump. What an embarrassment it had been when, during the election, they had let down the tyres of the Labour candidate's car and covered it with Tory posters! Someone would have to control them. Thinking of posters, he remembered with a smile the advice which Terry Lester had given him.

'Never deface one Labour poster this election. Much better idea. Our boys went round after the Labour wagons and took down the posters when they were still wet and then put them up again on shop windows, private houses, funeral undertakers and church notice boards. All the people came out in the morning and saw what these terrible Socialists had done! I told the Press I thought it was shocking. I gave out an official statement that if the Socialists didn't know the difference between a church notice board and a poster site, they had no right to be standing in the election.'

Wish I had someone like Terry on my Committee,

Gibley reflected. Wake them up a bit. Give these Labour boys some of their own medicine.

In addition to the special sections who were represented on the Executive, each municipal ward had two members. Some were quite decent, but others were impossible. Old Mr Crouch had joined only because he thought that membership would enable him to further his campaign for banning parking in Elmtree Avenue where he lived. And Mrs Glouster was firmly of the opinion that Upper Rossford was not the place it once was, ever since these new bungalows had been built at the top of the hill, and she caused acute embarrassment by talking about the 'scheme people', whenever the area was mentioned, as though they were an illiterate bunch of Hottentot refugees.

Some of his colleagues appeared to have helpful and friendly Executive Committees—Terry Lester talked about his as he would of real chums. But not him! Gibley was quite convinced that, if he had searched the length and breadth of the land, he could not have found a more disagreeable mob.

But all the members of this formidable body who had come to mind so far were, from his point of view, harmless types absorbed with their own sense of self-importance and the trivia of human existence, in comparison with that more malignant element in the body politic—his self-appointed 'straighteners'—who regarded it as their main purpose in life not only to keep their Member of Parliament on the narrow path of duty and loyalty to the Party line, but likewise pepped up to the proper degree of enthusiasm in pursuit of this. It was in this latter respect that—so it had been made fairly clear to Gibley in the past year or so—he was failing to match up. Loyalty personified, Gibley Horn was not of the stuff of which political rebels are made. Utterly devoid of the original sin of Party heresy, he had in the first place been a poor target for these people. Indeed, essentially a lazy-minded person, he found it a good deal easier to take the substance of his speeches from the helpful Party manuals that emanated from Central Office in such profusion, rather than attempt to make up any speech of his own. He had found that, provided he stuck closely to these, and interlarded his words with an occasional graceful tribute to the work of Party leaders, the prescription for a successful meeting was an infallible one.

The devotional ritual was accomplished, the litany had been intoned, those who had assembled to drink at the fountain of conformism had slaked their thirst, the hungry had been fed. All was well and the first half of his stay as M.P. for Rossford passed by in serene fashion: it was as if all critical elements were nonplussed at such excess of political virtue.

Including, so Gibley now thought rather bitterly, Bailie McMaw; during his first term as M.P., the Bailie had gradually become familiar to him as the thick-set figure with beetling brow and glowering mien who at every meeting sat at one end of the front row of the audience, ready and alert when it came for the time for discussion to set his seal of approval or disapproval on what had already been said. Gradually he had discovered the immense prestige of Bailie McMaw

in this assembly: man and boy, so it seemed, the Bailie
had worked for the Conservative Party in Rossford for
nigh on forty years and during that time he had
occupied every possible Office in the Association many
times over before retiring to his present prestigious
position as Life Vice-President. How fortunate it was,
thought Gibley during his early years, that, when the
Bailie did get up to speak, his words were invariably
favourable, almost unctuous indeed, in respect of the
loyalty of their 'new Member'. Perhaps, he considered,
the glower and the frown belied the real more equable
and kindly temper of the speaker.

It was only imperceptibly over the years that the
change started to occur:

'We have welcomed the words of our Member,' the
Bailie would invariably start, 'but,' he would clear his
throat, 'may we not have a wee bit of clarification . . .?'

Then would come the question for information that
would leave Gibley floundering in confusion. It was as
if the Bailie were calling his bluff and was only anxious
to expose the Member's total ignorance of any political
thought beyond the Party publications.

'Ah, well,' the Bailie would end, 'maybe if our
Member were a younger man with a more active brain,
he might have given us our answer?'

In course of time, Gibley came to dread the sight of
the Bailie sitting there, as he rose to speak. While the
latter's final sentence read like the knell of doom.
'Time to make way for a younger man,' was the phrase
that echoed in his brain from the statements of so many
of his colleagues about to retire. It was the last sort of

suggestion that he wanted to get around in the Rossford Division. He would have to show them that an older man, while retaining his energies, had also the advantage of acquired wisdom and mature judgment on which to rely in addition. Besides, he thought bitterly, who was the Bailie that he should hint of younger men in politics? He had been about the place long enough himself.

But then, of course, there was Miss Wotherspoon— Miss Janie Wotherspoon, Chairman for so long of the Women's Advisory Committee, still a representative on the Regional Council. Since her retirement from office three years previously Miss Wotherspoon had sat at the back of the meetings. Lean and with a slightly fanatical gleam in her eye, 'the Party' was never far from the lips and tongue of Miss Wotherspoon; and Gibley wondered perpetually how, by some alchemy which he never quite understood, the aims and interests of the great Conservative Party were made so frequently to correspond with the purely personal drives of Miss Wotherspoon herself—to obtain a little more power and influence for the Women's Committee, to bend the activities of the M.P. to her own wishes and desires, to ensure that her words were well reported in the local Press. Right from the start Gibley had felt an unease in the presence of this dangerous woman. This was not helped by the fact that, in the give and take of political conversation, she was a good deal quicker-witted than he was. He had managed to pacify this menacing two-legged creature during his early years by dancing with her at every possible occasion, whether at the Annual

Party Conference or at the local Ward 'hops' in Rossford. But even so, he had felt that he was working his passage the hard way: the years were slipping by and one could not dedicate the remainder of one's existence to dancing with Miss Wotherspoon. Whether this ungracious thought showed itself or whether there was a stirring in the breast of Miss Wotherspoon to the effect that, rather than have the portly and somewhat ungainly Gibley Horn for a dance partner as her M.P., there might possibly be a replacement, in these days when youth was coming into its own, by a more Adonis-like figure with quiffed hair and maybe wearing the dignified blue striped tie of the Old Etonian, it is difficult to say. But recently it had been a matter of common observation amongst Rossford Conservatives that the M.P. and the Women's Chairman were seen less frequently in each other's company; while there were now few occasions when Miss Wotherspoon did not take the opportunity to hymn the praises of the younger M.P.s in the House and the benefits which they were conferring on the Party by their presence in the House of Commons.

To think that he was travelling all this way from Westminster to Rossford to speak to them! He must be mad!

He was, he groaned to himself, merely 'the hired man'; but he had to keep in their good graces. They had given him the job in the first place and they could discard him at the drop of a hat, so to speak, and choose someone else for the next Election. A younger man, for instance. He shuddered at so uncomfortable a thought.

Of course, he mused, they did raise the cash to fight the Election and worked hard in doing so, although, truth to say, Gibley calculated that it would have been cheaper to pay the whole bill himself than to buy the hundreds of raffle tickets, tombola tokens, football cards and Derby Draw tickets which poured into 'Beechgrove' in a perpetual flood. And even if he won the odd scraggy hen in a raffle, it always had to be tactfully declined as was fitting for the Member of Parliament to do.

And what was he going to say to them tonight? The usual stuff, he supposed, though he would certainly tell them how that taxi-driver wasn't going to vote for the Labour Party ever again.

The journey was the usual grim ordeal and Gibley consumed three double gins which did not make him feel any better. Still, at least, the return journey would be by train.

But when he arrived at the Airport he felt distinctly groggy and not happy at the prospect of making a speech. Nevertheless, he got into his car and sped along the road to Rossford.

It was 7.50 p.m. when he arrived outside the Rossford Conservative Club where the meeting was to be held. Normally he went into the club-room for half an hour or so to wait for the Executive to do their normal business and chat to the ordinary members. But he did not fancy such social activity just now. Better wait a week or two and let time's soothing hand wipe out some of the more regrettable aspects of the week-end Press stories. Instead, he would go for a short walk; but after going along the High Street for a few yards he saw the welcoming glow from the 'Thorn and Thistle' and decided that another gin and tonic—or perhaps he would make it a rum and ginger wine on a cold evening like this—was just what he needed to give him the confidence necessary to meet his Executive.

He did not know any of the three gentlemen who were seated at the table in the corner, but one of them greeted him in a friendly manner with the announcement that a television star was in their midst. Basically of a convivial nature, Gibley decided to join them and, recognising that they all knew precisely who he was, he felt obliged to seek their opinions on his performance on the small box.

'You were terrible! Disastrous!' said the most scruffy-looking chap in the group, who clearly did not appreciate that gentlemen should remove their headgear when within a building.

'That's no way to talk to Mr Horn,' his colleague rebuked him. 'It must be bloody difficult with these bright lights shining on you. I think you were just great,' he assured Gibley, 'even if you did look a wee bit daft. Let me buy you a drink.'

Gibley assured the gentleman that he was well provided already, but a refusal was impossible. And so another rum arrived at Gibley's hand. And the conversation ranged round a wide field including the prospects of the local football team and the high price of haircuts. If anyone was swindled at the hairdresser it was himself, Gibley assured them, pointing to his shining bald head, and his companions immediately appreciated that a sound wit was one of the attributes of their M.P., which they had never previously been aware of. They laughed heartily and one of them gave Gibley a forceful slap on the back to confirm that they were now all friends together. It would have been less than gracious of Gibley to depart without inviting these three jolly chaps to partake of his hospitality and they willingly accepted. The third gentleman then announced that he would be a poor constituent indeed were he not to take the opportunity of buying his own M.P. a drink and, despite Gibley's protests, the constituent's honour was saved through the purchase of another round.

The clock on the wall showed that it was 8.25 p.m. and, fortified by four times the quantity of confidence which he had considered necessary on entering the 'Thorn and Thistle', Gibley departed for the Conservative Club feeling in much better humour. He would tell the Committee just what the position was! He would put them in their place if they cut up rough. They had it coming to them! Who were they to tell him what to do and what not to do!

An agitated Alec Anderson was waiting for him in the vestibule.

'Where have you been?' he inquired anxiously. 'We finished our business at 8.20 p.m. Thought you would have made an effort to be in good time tonight. You've no idea what some of them were saying before the meeting.'

'Won't do them any harm to wait,' Gibley assured his Agent in a slow and ponderous drawl. 'Let'm cool down.' The 'cool' took as long to say as Gibley would normally take for an average sentence and, after the 'oo' sound had taken five seconds to deliver, Alec gathered that either Gibley had hidden reserves of confidence or else that he had been adding to his liquid assets in the most obvious manner. At other times he would have respectfully suggested that the M.P. might care to have a quick wash under the cold tap, but the Executive members were already in an agitated state and Alec had no wish to offend the people who paid his wages and were shortly going to receive an application for an increase in his miserable stipend.

'Better come right away,' he said anxiously, while firmly declining Gibley's offer of refreshment in the Club Bar.

'Ta-a-ke your time,' said Gibley sonorously, and walked with carefully placed steps behind his Agent.

Normally when Gibley entered an Executive Meeting there was a ripple of applause which made his journey to the platform a little less embarrassing but, when he now entered the packed room, he immediately perceived that the members were in no mind to give their customary greeting. This annoyed him and he was not prepared to let the matter rest there.

'No clapping?' he inquired pugnaciously, and looked with such hostility at Miss Janie Wotherspoon in the back row that, momentarily taken aback, she was persuaded to start beating her hands together, which demonstration was taken up automatically by the ladies sitting beside her.

'That's better,' said Gibley with no little pomposity,

and strode through the seated crowd towards the platform where Major Perkins was occupying the middle chair of three, with a handful of papers, a large jug of water and glass on the table separating him from the audience.

As he sat down in the chair on the Chairman's right, Gibley seized the quarter-pint tumbler and proceeded to pour about one-third of a pint into it, causing no small overflow, and swallowed the tumblerful with a mighty gulp.

Sitting back in the chair with a satisfied look on his face, he permitted himself to utter a substantial belch which astonished the by-now-puzzled audience.

''Scuse me,' he greeted the Chairman politely. 'It's the done thing in India. But this isn't India.' Gibley was surprised that none of the members joined in his laughter at this splendid jest, but he did not restrain his own mirth on account of their dull wit.

'What's keeping you?' he asked the Chairman anxiously, but nevertheless publicly. 'The show must go on!'

Major Perkins was horrified by the events which had preceded this. A strong and pungent odour of rum was coming in waves from the M.P. He never liked taking the Chair at meetings and was extremely put out by the slightest deviation from the normal. But this was not a deviation. It was a disaster. And he was too confused to know what to do.

Members of an audience always know that speakers will be nervous, apprehensive and unsure; but nobody ever spares a thought for the poor Chairman. Agonies of doubt were never far from Major Perkins's mind, but this happening had quite paralysed him.

'Get on with it,' came an impatient shout from Gibley, now feeling the equal of ten of the Major and he reinforced his view by a sharp prod. And so Major Perkins got on with it.

'Ladies and Gentleman,' he began, 'we have with us tonight our Member of Parliament, Mr Gibley Horn.'

'They can all see that,' said Gibley, in the mood for merry jests.

'And . . . and he has come up from Westminster specially to speak to you . . .'

'To address them,' Gibley corrected him. It was tiresome to have such a dull-witted Chairman.

'Please be silent when I'm speaking,' the Major whispered in an agitated voice, the friendly bonds established at the dinner the previous night already having been severed.

'Well, get on with it. We haven't got all night. I'm the speaker, not you.'

It was some considerable time since the Major had been so insulted. He was getting thoroughly fed up and would have sat down at once had his wife not been present. She always gave him an objective summary of his performance as Chairman after each meeting, and life was a lot easier for him if he conducted himself well.

'The Member seems to think that I am talking too much,' he continued, hoping that a touch of humour would break the evil spell which seemed to have been cast on the meeting.

'Hear, hear!' confirmed Gibley enthusiastically.

'And so I will just call upon him to speak and to answer your questions.' The Major sat down looking confused and saw, for the first time, that his carefully collected papers were lying in front of him in a soggy state from the water which Gibley had spilled. This annoyed him even more and he took out his handkerchief and proceeded to wipe the papers vigorously.

'It seems that our Chairman's a little wet,' Gibley began, and was immediately annoyed at the audience for refusing to appreciate this telling *double entendre*. He stepped forward to emphasise his point and only with difficulty prevented himself from falling forward even farther.

'Almost fell then.' But he was stating the obvious. Three ladies in the front seat assumed that look of anxiety which is the common lot of those who live in anticipation of a portly Member of Parliament descending on to their laps.

'Falling fever!' he advised them. 'But you won't know anything about that! It's still secret. But soon the whole wide world will know about falling fever. I'm going to tell them.'

Gibley stepped back to let this dramatic news sink in.

At this point young George Alexander, who took great delight in raising points of order and tedious little constitutional points on every occasion, decided that it was time for him to take action. He was a person of considerable importance, being Vice-Chairman of the Young Conservatives. And he would be Chairman next year if Jim Ross married the present Chairman, Jean Hazleden, and took her away to his new job down

South. He had never liked the idea of having Mr Horn
as the M.P. and had even felt qualms of conscience
when he had put a large black cross against Gibley's
name on the ballot paper at the last Election. He might
have hesitated further, but for the fact that his father
had come with him to vote and, despite all the notices
signifying that the ballot was secret, the parent had
stood over his son and said, 'Horn. That's the Tory
man. Put the cross there. No, not there, silly. There!'

But it seemed tonight that the M.P. was, to say the
least of it, a little unwell and George knew that there
must be some constitutional point to cover such an
eventuality.

'On a point of Order, Major Perkins,' he began . . .
but he was not permitted to continue.

'I don't allow little twerps to interrupt me,' Gibley
hastened to assure Mr Alexander. 'Don't you learn
manners at school any more?'

Major Perkins had to admit to himself that it was an
ill wind . . . because Gibley had done just what the
Major had been longing to do for many meetings, and
the astonished look on George's face, as he hastily
resumed his seat, strengthened the Major's resolve to
silence the young so-and-so the next time he tried to
draw attention to paragraph 17 (a) of the Constitution
of the Association.

A hushed murmur of frenzied conversation had followed George Alexander's intervention and Gibley felt
obliged to shout 'Silence!' with his new-found confidence. And silence reigned.

'Must tell you about the taxi-driver I met tonight.'

It was now time to proceed to serious political discussion. . . .

'Voted Labour all his life.' A long pause to let that sink in.

'But I had a word with him tonight.' Another long pause to emphasise the magnitude of the privilege which the taxi-driver had enjoyed.

'And he's going to vote for the jolly old Conservatives next time.' Gibley conveyed this important news with a flourish and was depressed to find that his own enthusiasm was not of the infectious sort.

'I've been so busy,' he continued. 'So, so, so busy. You don't know what a hard life we have in Parlmnt (the contraction was his own). Always on the go. Always rushing up to speak at meetings. You don't appreciate me. But I work very, very, very hard.'

At this point the continual references to the heavy duties which he was carrying on behalf of the citizens of Rossford made Gibley feel very tired and he slumped down in his chair and looked sorrowful.

Major Perkins, looking more miserable than ever, got to his feet and mumbled, 'Are there any questions?' clearly conveying his hope that there were none.

Most of the Executive members were conscious of the Major's difficulty and desisted from asking any questions. But George Alexander had by now recovered from his humiliation and decided that a question would redeem his position. He sprang to his feet.

'I should like to know what the Member thinks about the present situation in the Amerbala Coastal Strip with specific reference to the sending of Dr Iffenzi to the Seychelles, and what steps the Member thinks should be taken to restore harmony and constitutional government to the area?'

This would not have been a difficult question at any ordinary time. But in Gibley's elated state it was a gift.

'I thought I told you to be quiet,' he reminded George sternly. 'But I'm going to answer your question. Lock them all up. That's what we should do.'

He sat down, confident that his answer had fully covered the obvious points. George was all for following the matter up, but a wildly hostile glare from Major Perkins convinced young Mr Alexander that the welfare of the residents of Amerbala would require to be considered further at a more appropriate time—as would that of Mr Gibley Horn.

'Our M.P. has told me that he would have to leave us early in time to catch his train,' the Chairman announced with a sigh of relief. But suddenly sensing signs of agitation at his side, added, 'and we must thank Mr Horn for coming all the way from London to address us.'

A ripple of applause—or was it relief—greeted this announcement.

'Not very hearty, are they?' Gibley asked the Chairman.'

Sensing from the Chairman's face that fireworks were about to commence and knowing where his duty lay, Alec Anderson stepped forward and prodded Gibley till he moved in the direction of the side door just off the platform. Gibley protested. But, without hesitating, Alec escorted the M.P. along the corridor and guided him to his car.

As they went out of the door, a familiar sound caught their ears—it was that of Bailie McMaw clearing his throat prior to addressing the body of the Hall.

Alec quickly obtained the keys for the car and drove Gibley to the station where, fortunately, the sleeper train was already in the platform. Gibley was taken by Alec to his compartment and placed, fully clothed, in bed. Alec had a quiet word with the understanding attendant and took a taxi back to Rossford in the hope that he could have a word with the Chairman before he left the Club. He suspected, correctly, that Major Perkins would stay on for a few drinks after his ordeal.

❊❊❊　　❊❊❊　　❊❊❊

When Gibley wakened at Euston station the next morning, he was conscious mainly of having a splitting headache. He remembered only a little of what had transpired the previous evening, but such episodes as he did recall filled him with gloom. What an idiot he had been! What on earth would Major Perkins and the Executive Committee do now? He could well imagine. How was he going to face them ever again?

❊❊❊　　❊❊❊　　❊❊❊

A glass of salts and a breakfast consisting of black coffee reinforced the effects of the wash in cold water to which he had subjected himself on reaching the hotel. He still felt pretty wretched and, when he let his thoughts stray back to the previous evening, it did not improve his sense of well-being.

What in earth had got into him? he thought. He knew that, although he had never had a reputation of being brilliant, he had always been regarded as being an upholder of everything that was decent and honourable in the constituency. He had even given a talk on the virtues of temperance at the White Hope Guild Meeting. There had never been any personal scandal about him. But what ammunition he had provided his critics with now! He doubted if he could survive this disaster.

But, if an election was called soon and he was not readopted, what in earth was he going to do for money? Apart from the size of his salary as an M.P., which was not great when you considered the outlay, there was the question of the credit which the salary could create. He could never carry on with a £600 overdraft if he was deprived of his job. And there was little he could turn his hand to. He cursed his lack of foresight. He should have been much more assiduous in seeking out directorships. He should have tried to do a bit of writing for newspapers. That first article, which had taken him four days to write, had not been accepted by the editor of the weekly paper who had commissioned him, but perhaps if he had persevered he might have got somewhere.

Now it was a time of crisis. A time for decision. What could he do?

As he sipped his last cup of coffee Gibley resolved that there was no merit in crying over spilt milk or thinking about the past. He could only overcome his troubles if he cast them out of his mind and started anew to work hard and thoroughly. He would have to put down lots of Questions in the House. He would have to make more speeches. While circumstances would make it embarrassing to do much constituency work for the next few weeks, he would have to try to do the rounds during the recesses. Plenty of school visits and factories. That was the answer. He would start anew.

He had meant to do just that on many occasions before and never achieved it. But he had never been faced with such a serious crisis. Surely the sheer extent of the emergency would itself strengthen his resolve.

The first opportunity—the real test—would come this very morning. It was Tuesday and, as usual, the Scottish Grand Committee would be meeting at 10.30 a.m. Or was it the Scottish Standing Committee? For the moment, he forgot which. However, Gibley knew that he was a member of whatever it was and would have to attend.

The Grand Committee was when every single Scottish Member, as well as some English Conservatives (brought in to redress the balance and preserve a Government majority) met together to discuss a Scottish Bill. The English Members disliked being put on this Committee as it forced them to sit through a morning's debate when those whom they considered to be long-winded Scotsmen would spend hours discussing fish-meal factories in Fife or cart tracks in Caithness. To be put on the Scottish Grand Committee was regarded by the English membership of the British legislature rather as members of the Russian equivalent would view a transfer to Siberia. The Whips, on the other hand, regarded the Committee as a splendid means of keeping the newer members out of mischief and of reminding them forcibly that Parliament business did not consist exclusively of turning the world upside down or making major decisions of constitutional importance.

The Scottish Standing Committee was much smaller —consisting of about twenty-five Scottish Members drawn from the Parties in line with the division of their representation in the House. The Liberals were always complaining that they could only get one Member on the Scottish Standing Committee and the lone Nationalist was annoyed that he never got on to it at all. 'According to this nonsensical English arrangement,' he explained on T.V., 'even if we won every one of Scotland's seventy-one seats, we could only get, at the most, three members on Scotland's own Standing Committee. I have put down a Motion on the subject,' he explained, as if to show that bloody revolution would only come as a last resort.

With the relatively small number of Tories in Scotland (even although there were more than last time) Gibley always seemed to be included in both Committees, and his Tuesday and Thursday mornings were always, therefore, 'booked' for most weeks of Parliament.

And what was the Committee talking about just now? Housing subsidies, he thought, because he could remember Archie Dundas having made an impassioned speech last week about slums in his constituency. Never used to hear him much when their crowd were in power, Gibley reflected darkly. But, with the advent of another Conservative Government, the responsibility for bad housing had suddenly become the fault of the Government again.

Gibley remembered that one of the new Glasgow Tories had been shouting about the Labour Government's terrible housing record about three months ago and he had quoted lots of facts and figures. He would have to look this up in the Library. The chappie had proved conclusively, much to the satisfaction of Gibley's slow intellect, that these terrible slums in Glasgow and elsewhere were entirely the fault of the Labour Party. This pleasing news had cheered Gibley considerably at the time and he resolved to have another look at the 'proof'.

'What date did young Peterson make that speech with masses of figures about Scottish housing?' he asked the librarian, and a careful search through the records showed the date was in July. Gibley just had time to go and get a copy of the relevant Hansard before the Committee started at 10.30 a.m.

As he looked round the Committee room, he saw that there were only seventeen members there—so it must be the Standing Committee. And he saw that the Opposition benches were very full—all looking eagerly at the Chairman as though he was about to fire a gun for the start of a race up Ben Nevis.

Half past ten struck. The Chairman rose to announce the business. Everyone knew that the business was the Committee stage of the Housing Subsidies Bill—a small blue document with 18 pages and 39 clauses.

But for those who had not followed the Committee's proceedings carefully, the Chairman explained with a sigh that consideration of Clause 2 had been completed and the next business was 'page 2, Clause 3, line 18, in place of "may" insert "shall" '. He then called upon Mr Dundas to move this earth-shaking amendment. It was clear, when Archie rose to speak, that he would require some considerable time to outline the arguments in favour of this alteration and that several of his colleagues would also require time to back up his case.

It had already taken eight sittings over four weeks to get through the mass of amendments to Clauses 1 and 2 and, if progress went on at this slow rate, it was clear that afternoon and evening sittings—perhaps sittings through the whole night—would be needed to get the legislation through. The fact that the Labour Party did not like the Bill had been apparent for some time. By moving a host of amendments to each and every clause, they had in mind to delay its progress or at least to have a goodly number of rows and scenes during its passage. The bold type of that frequent headline 'Scots M.P.s in Commons Storm' would have to be kept in readiness for at least another ten Tuesdays and Thursdays.

The Rossford M.P. had only a dim awareness of this —he usually spent his time in Committee in answering his correspondence—but he did know that the Bill had been discussed for a very long time and he hoped that he could at least have the opportunity of making a speech. It would have to be on this amendment, if he was going to speak today. Better to find out what it was all about.

So he looked up page 2 and scanned the page till he

came to line 18. It was the first line of Clause 3 which read, 'The Secretary of State may, without prejudice to the provisions of Clause 2, pay a subsidy not exceeding £7 per annum in respect of houses contained in buildings of between 5 and 6 storeys.'

And Archie Dundas wanted to change the word 'may' to 'shall'. Better listen to what he had to say, and see what holes he could pick in his arguments.

'It was a scandalous waste of the Committee's time,' Archie explained to sarcastic cries of 'Hear, hear' from the Government benches who regarded him as the greatest filibuster on God's earth, 'to spend so much time on this clause which offers only such a miserable and tiny subsidy.' But, it seemed according to Archie, that local Councils might be deprived of even this meagre pittance by the Government who, under the Bill, were not forced to pay the £7. It would only be paid if the Government chose to pay it. And if, as probably would be said, the Government had every intention of paying the subsidy, why could they not put in the word 'shall' and reassure the local authorities who did not have a great deal of trust in the Government's motives.

And what was the idea of a subsidy for houses of five and six storeys? Was the Government trying to discourage multi-storey building? Were they endeavouring to hold up progress? Were their heads buried in the sand? And would this not further impede the housing drive and deprive more families, living in poor and squalid conditions, of the bright new and sunny homes which were their rightful entitlement?

7

When a Tory member interrupted Archie to point out, politely, that house-building figures were leaping ahead under the new Government, Archie explained haughtily that the Labour Government had devoted their energies to building great hunks of multi-storey blocks which they had not quite finished when leaving office, and the Tories had just come in, put on the top storey and shouted 'Eureka' or whatever Tories say when happy—'We've built hundreds of houses!'

This was regarded as the tall story of the year by the Tories present and their loud laughter produced angry shouts and denials from the Opposition. Tom Crossley, who never made speeches but maintained a constant stream of interruptions, shook his fist at the Tory benches and suggested to the Conservative who had made the point that his noble head, far from being filled with factual information, was full of mince! And this provoked the kind of scene which is invariably described as 'Commons uproar' in the Press.

The Chairman allowed tempers to exercise themselves a bit and then rose with dignity to remind Members that the only issue before them was whether the word 'shall' should be substituted for 'may' on line 18 of page 2 and proposed, respectfully, that their minds should be directed only to this proposition.

Alistair Mackintosh, the Scottish Government Whip, went scurrying round to his colleague who had provoked Tom Crossley, and explained to him that such interjections simply served to lengthen the proceedings and the primary objective was to get the Bill through as speedily as possible. This did not make sound sense to his colleague who considered that he had made a telling point, but he agreed to restrain himself in future as far as possible. Gibley took the opportunity to prod Alistair when he was passing and say that he would like to make a little speech that morning. A look of horror came across the Whip's face. He explained, as courteously as he could, that the Government were most anxious to complete Clause 3 that very day and that a speech from Gibley was just the kind of thing which could keep them all discussing 'may' and 'shall' for days to come. The Whip was sincere in this because, on the few occasions Gibley spoke in Committee, he had an unfortunate failing of being provoked into angry exchanges by the constant stream of interruptions from the other side and, in their present mood, the Labour boys would have a field day.

'Some other time,' he pleaded quietly, 'but please *not* today!'

If Gibley had been more of a rebel he would have told the Whip to go and jump. Being a true loyalist, he agreed to this proposal. His splendid speech could wait till Thursday. What difference would two days make when he was going to turn over a new leaf? And, to be quite truthful, he did not altogether fancy making a speech when the Opposition was in such fighting fettle. So he decided instead to go out for a cup of coffee in the corridor where he would listen alertly for the cry of 'Division in Room 14' which would send him scurrying back to cast his vote.

But the call to greatness did not come till noon. As he came back to the Committee room, the Whip

grabbed him and advised him that there would be two
votes and that the first was 'Aye'. Even after all these
years, Gibley never quite understood how it was that
when they were wanting to turn down a Labour
Amendment they should shout 'Aye', nor did he follow
all this stuff which the Chairman was saying about the
question being 'that the word proposed to be left out
stand part of the clause'. But he did what he was told
and dutifully shouted 'Aye' when his name was called.

The Committee then moved on to the next amendment which, again on line 18, proposed to substitute
the word 'of' for the words 'not exceeding'. And, this
time, Hugh McKay was entrusted with the task of
leading the Opposition attack.

Soon it was one o'clock and the Committee was
adjourned. Gibley and the other Members stamped out
noisily, knowing that they would now have to wait
till Thursday before they knew whether this significant Bill would have the word 'of' or the words 'not
exceeding' in line 18 of page 2. As he left, Gibley found
himself again in the company of the Whip.

'I'm so grateful to you, Gibley,' the latter said
effusively. 'The Chief is *so* anxious to finish this Bill by
the end of the month and this means the maximum of
co-operation from our own Members. It must be
galling to hear these Labour people talking such nonsense and not be able to come in and squash them. But
if we took every opportunity to correct them we would
be here till Christmas! I really am most grateful for
your help!'

'Hm,' mumbled Gibley. So it appeared that speeches

on this Bill were out. He wouldn't even be able to make that grand speech on Thursday. That was a nuisance. He would have to concentrate on the House itself to make his big come-back. That was irritating, but at least there was plenty of time to hit the headlines before the next election. 'Rome wasn't built in a day.' Nor would be the new Gibley Horn.

❈❈❈   ❈❈❈   ❈❈❈

He tramped down from the Committee Room and went to the Post Office to collect his mail. The usual stuff again and he would just keep it in his brief-case till tomorrow morning when he had booked a session with Mrs Milligan at the Agency. She was a pleasant and efficient person and Gibley had let her share the personal distresses which the Rossford electors communicated to him for the ten years he had been in the House. By a private arrangement, Mrs Milligan also co-operated in answering phone calls for him. When, not wishing to admit that he carried on his activities without a private secretary, a message was to come to the House he simply advised the caller to telephone his 'Secretary', Mrs Milligan, at extension 413. He had even gone to the length of giving her name to the Whips Office so that any messages about his pairing arrangements or from the Clerks in the Table Office would go to her direct. Then Mrs Milligan would write out a letter in her delicate hand and put it on the message board for him.

He was glad to see that there was a bulky envelope from the Insect Friendship League and a careful

7*

scrutiny of the contents showed that, apart from a long-winded and enthusiastic epistle of gratitude from Miss Phillimore, there were two or three typed reports and some Press cuttings. One of them would no doubt be Professor Himmelstein's Presidential Address. The reading of this could be delayed for a while. But he was interested to see that, among the papers, was a letter which Miss Phillimore had sent to the Minister of Science outlining the League's alarm and despondency at the effect of insecticides on the cornfields of Paraguay and Britain and the devastating consequences which this would have for the entire population. She suggested that another Parliamentary Question might be put down about this stirring letter and, in his new active frame of mind, Gibley considered that this was a good idea. He was going to put down lots of Questions from now on, but it was so difficult to know just what to ask. Here, at least, was a suitable subject and it might give him more information about the effects of BX20 before his big debate. So he grabbed a bit of paper from the rack in the Post Office and wrote down carefully but rather illegibly (because his glasses were in his brief-case and the effort to get them out was just too much):

'Mr Gibley Horn to ask the Minister of Science what information he has received from the I.F.L. regarding the growth and treatment of cereal crops and if he will make a statement about the consequences for the population of the world.'

He hoped that the Clerks would be able to read his rather indecipherable scrawl, but if they did not make it out they could always ask him. And he carefully marked the Question with a star to show that he wanted an oral answer. Remembering that the Minister of Science now answered questions on a Monday he put down the date of the following Monday on top of the Question.

He walked along to the Table Office and found Mr Colquhoun, one of the younger men, in the office.

'There's a Question for the Minister of Science,' he explained. 'I want an oral answer.' And he threw the question into the basket. Normally, the Clerk would look over the question to see that it was in order or to question any bad writing. But Gibley did not look with favour on the prospect of having to explain that the whole thing was about Spotted Hummerflies and the like, so he simply said that if there were any points to raise the Clerk could drop him a note.

He then decided, in a fresh burst of energy, that he would have to go up and give a copy of his Bill to the Bill Office staff. So he climbed up the stairs and went into this Parliamentary boffins' lair at the top of the building.

'There's my Private Bill,' said Gibley as he passed over the copy. 'I know it looks a bit daft, but there are some big things behind it all.'

The Clerk looked at the Bill with an astonished frown and clearly was not immediately aware of the significant matters which could be raised under the umbrella of the Spotted Hummerfly Protection Bill, but he saw that the Member for Rossford was in no

mood for a discussion on its merits. He hastened, however, to advise Gibley that the first reading of the
Private Bills would take place the following Tuesday
and that his big day would probably come soon after
the Christmas recess.

Back in the Table Office young Mr Colquhoun was
looking curiously at Gibley's question. What information has the Minister received from what body? Was
that an 'F' or an 'R' or a 'P'? He looked up a register
of organisations and saw nothing under I.F.L. The
Insect League was not considered to be significant
enough to be included in the list. I.P.L.? Yes, there
was an International Physical Laboratory financed by
the Government and operating in Cornwall. It came
under the Ministry of Science. That was probably
what the Member was after, but he would have to
make sure. Oral Question, Mr Horn had stated. The
first chance of an Oral Question to the Minister would
be the 28th February. Better tell him that.

So he wrote out a little postcard inviting the Rossford
M.P. to come and consult the Clerks about his
Question. And he speedily dismissed the whole matter
from his mind.

While at lunch, Gibley heard the alarming news that
the sitting that day could probably be a very long one.
How he hated these all-night sittings! Just as he was getting to sleep in an armchair in the Library the Division
Bell would ring and they would all have to march along
to go through the Lobbies. He always smoked too much
and could guarantee a splitting headache by morning.
Why couldn't they arrange business more sensibly?

As the day progressed, it became clear that the sitting was indeed going to be a long one. The Committee Stage of the Development Districts Special Relief Bill was being taken as a Committee of the whole House and not upstairs in Committee. There was no way in which the Opposition's speeches could be limited apart from the 'Closure' and the Speaker did not allow that until there had been a full discussion of each clause.

Every Labour Member representing a seat in a Development Area seemed anxious to make a speech and they all looked intent on showing how the Bill would not deal in any way with the very special problems in their constituencies. All stuff for the local Press, thought Gibley, and strode out of the Chamber.

Rossford was, of course, a Development Area and the thought suddenly came to Gibley that if he went to the Library and did a bit of research, he might make a speech later that night. By midnight, the daily newspapers' reporters ceased to show any real interest in the proceedings, but a speech even at 6 a.m. was reported in Hansard and could be sent on to the local papers for publication. Just the thing, thought Gibley, with the *Rossford Gazette* in mind.

But, before he started on his studies, he decided that a word with the Whips would be advisable. They were not enthusiastic. In fact they were definitely horrified at the prospect of any backbencher from the Government side holding up the proceedings. It would be difficult enough to get the Committee Stage through by the next morning and, if there was any unforeseen delay, they would be presented with the alternatives of allowing another valuable day for the Bill or losing the business for the following day. Gibley could never quite see the argument about losing a valuable day when the House took four months' holiday each year, but the Whips were so insistent that he decided not to press this point.

It is never easy to find adequate entertainment in any place under the sun between the hours of 2.30 a.m. and 11 a.m. And the House of Commons is the last place in the world in which suitable recreation can be found for such a long period. The only possibilities were the Library which was filled with heavily bound books which scared off all save the scholarly, the tea-room which churned out gallons of tea and coffee throughout the night, the bars which dispensed a wider selection of liquid sustenance and a chess room where a small group of experts played this game with deep absorption until cobwebs provided them with a covering cloak.

For Gibley the only possibilities were the Library where the splendid cosy easy chairs were conducive to sleep and the bar where some pleasing gossip could usually be exchanged.

Sleep did not come easily to him that night. The deep snores and grunts from his fellow students in the Library stood in the way of his journey to slumber and he spent most of the night, between votes, in one of the bars or in tramping out on to the Terrace for the breath of air which would be guaranteed to keep him awake, if not entirely conscious.

Daybreak came and he felt distinctly ill and groggy. And when the final Division took place at 11 a.m. he felt worse. Wednesday was not such a bad day and his attendance would not be required until 10 p.m. So he decided to make speedily for his hotel where a warm bed would be waiting for him. As he scurried through the Lobby he was handed a message advising him that Mrs Milligan of the Agency would appreciate a few words on the phone.

He had forgotten all about this engagement with his secretary, and realised that apologies were called for.

Mrs Milligan was most understanding as Gibley conveyed his apologies through the rather noisy line, the crackles of which failed to coincide with the drumbeats in his head.

'Before you go,' Mrs Milligan advised, 'The Table Office were on the phone about that Question. An Oral Answer will mean putting it off till February 28th.'

'O.K.!' He felt he would do anything to end the conversation and get away to bed.

'And it *was* the Laboratory, wasn't it?' the gentle voice persisted.

Gibley had no idea what this was all about, but decided that a firm 'yes' would terminate the conversation more speedily than any questioning of what particular laboratory Mrs Milligan had suddenly taken an interest in.

'I'll phone back and tell them,' assured Mrs Milligan. 'Have a good sound sleep and I'll see you again on Thursday afternoon. That's tomorrow,' she added, lest in his confusion Gibley had lost track of the days.

The conversation ended. Gibley took a cab to the hotel and within twenty minutes was dead to the world.

That evening, as he wandered into the House at 9.30 p.m., feeling considerably better after a good sleep, but having a funny impression that the clocks were wrong, he was depressed to find in his mail a stiff note from Major Perkins.

'Dear Horn,' it began.

That was bad for a start. While the pair had never actually been on first name terms apart from the odd occasion when the Major let his natural reticence go, the worst salutation so far had been 'Dear Gibley Horn'. And the letters had never ended with a less friendly greeting than 'Yours sincerely', but here was the conclusion in the unfriendly terms of 'Yours faithfully—A. Perkins'. And below the typed message 'Chairman, Rossford Conservative Association' to remove any doubts that the letter was written in his official capacity.

'I should be grateful if you will make a point of contacting me by telephone on your return to the Constituency at the week-end.'

The message was plain and unambiguous, but Gibley appreciated that, hidden behind this invitation, lurked dark hints of trouble to come.

For the rest of the week, even during his train journey to Rossford on Thursday night, he was conscious that the proposed telephone conversation would not be taken by the Major as an opportunity to exchange sentiments of goodwill and fellowship. The fact that Alec Anderson had not even written to him or telephoned during the whole week confirmed his view that the main forces of Party officialdom were now ranged against him.

When he arrived home the cool reception he received from Margaret indicated that, somehow or other, she had heard disturbing rumours about the conduct of her husband at the Executive Committee meeting. True, she had had no specific report of the proceedings, but Miss Wotherspoon had telephoned her on Tuesday morning to ask if her husband was keeping quite well and Margaret Horn had immediately grasped the fact that the lady's apparent concern must have stemmed from Gibley's activities the previous evening.

'Acted a little strangely', was the most that she could get out of Miss Wotherspoon, but the implication had clearly been that Gibley had been plastered.

Even when Gibley had indicated, in his usual casual manner, that there was 'nothing to worry about', Margaret sensed with the intuition that all good wives possess that the worries were both considerable and alarming.

Nor had she been heartened to hear snippets of the telephone conversation which Gibley had been privileged to enjoy with Major Perkins.

The Major had been more alarmed than impressed with the Member's assurances that a new chapter was about to commence and that Rossford people would, from now on, find it difficult to lift a newspaper without seeing a further example of their M.P. fighting furiously for some excellent cause.

He had also been left cold by Gibley's description of the Private Bill which he would be introducing shortly and which, he alleged, could well save humanity from a slow and lingering death.

The gist of the Major's message was that the performance on Monday night had gravely aggravated the dissatisfaction which many of the Executive members had felt about their M.P. for some time, and that the sporting thing for old Gibley to do in the circumstances was to make the supreme sacrifice and wipe the dust of Rossford from his clumsy feet before the next Election came along.

There was no doubt about the dissatisfaction which had been there before. The plain fact was that the good people of the Committee were a little tired of Gibley. After ten years in the House, he had not risen through the ranks. The Marshal's baton was still resting in his Private's haversack and there seemed to be little chance of its ever being unpacked. Nor did Gibley have the fulsome charm with which other backbenchers compensated their Committees in the absence of promotion. Gibley was also lacking in any distinction which could sweeten the pill. He was not an Admiral or a Major-General and he did not even have the meagre consolation of a title. When Mrs Cole-Pratt went along to the Regional Ladies Executive she felt in the position of being landed with an idiot boy, while the other ladies had brilliant children to display.

She had no counter ammunition when Mrs Buchanan-Prentice crowed about the 'wonderful cocktail Party which the Admiral had held' and at which 'everyone' had been present. And she was again reduced to stony silence when Mrs Molketer spoke proudly about her Member's splendid performance in the Ministry of Agriculture. 'Gets on splendidly with Sir Oliver.' 'A future Prime Minister the *Argosy* predicted.' Gibley Horn had no telling triumphs to compete with that lot.

'It was time for the Rossford M.P. to make room for a younger man'—so indeed the sinister rumours started to be whispered about.

However, decency and decorum prevented any action being taken to dump their Member, but the events of Monday had provided just the opportunity which had been lacking, and Mrs Cole-Pratt, Miss Wotherspoon and their friends were certainly going to strike when the iron was hot and while the rum vapours could still be sniffed in their memories.

'Think that you should let it be known that you're not standing again,' the Major suggested but, having a touching faith in the effect of the new leaf which he was about to turn, Gibley insisted that he would need a couple of months to think it over.

As a cautious insurance, he had a further chat with Margaret about this little hotel in the Highlands which would provide relief and sanctuary from the cruel world of politics, and Gibley was surprised to find how enthusiastic his wife was about the whole business. Again, they determined that they would 'save like mad'. And once again Gibley wrote out on a long sheet of paper the ideal monthly budget which, if adhered to strictly, would enable them to collect the nest egg with which a small hotel could be financed.

But gloom was never far away that week-end and, when he left again for London on Monday, he felt extremely sad and almost indifferent to his fate.

On Tuesday he would have to present his Bill and, thereafter, any M.P.s or outside bodies who wished to read it would be able to do so. Professor Himmelstein had written to say that he would have to be present on this historic occasion and Gibley had been able to get him a seat in the Gallery.

On the appointed day the Clerk carefully lined up the M.P.s behind the Speaker's Chair as the hour approached and then, one by one, in the order in which their names had emerged from the box, the M.P.s advanced with the Bills in their hands.

Mr Paul Maxwell was announced and he stepped forward and passed his Bill to the Clerk.

'House Conversion Advisory Commission Bill,' the Clerk read out. This was no surprise and was simply a means of further ventilating the argument which had caused Terry Lester such concern.

'Mr Iain Cochrane.' Wonder what he would choose?

'Aliens Alimony Bill.' No doubt something which one of these funny foreign bodies had asked him to push forward. Probably the rectification of some anomaly which would stop Dutchmen running away to South America and leaving their wives parked in London to be looked after by the Welfare State.

'Mr Gibley Horn.' Here it came!

'Spotted Hummerfly Protection Bill.' The Clerk seemed to reserve his most haughty and dignified voice for this one: a titter of amusement went round the benches.

'Fancy old Gibley being taken in by these fresh air and nutmeg loonies,' he could almost hear them saying.

But he would show them all. Make them sit up indeed. Just wait until he told them about that BX20 stuff. And the 'falling fever'. And how the Americans were using Britain as a testing ground. He would certainly show them!

During that week he spent every spare moment consulting books and magazines in the Commons Library and studying every possible reference which he could find to insecticides and insects. He also took every opportunity to advise his colleagues of the information he had discovered and to seek their support for his Bill when it came up. He had a word with David Forbes, the Liberal, and John Knox-Crichton to remind them forcibly of the duty of sponsors of a Bill to collect as much support as they could. He had a go at old Will Francis, but the latter seemed to have entirely forgotten not only that he was a sponsor of the Bill, but even that he had recently discussed it with Gibley. And the Rossford M.P. departed from Will impatiently and without even waiting to hear the end of that story about how, back in the thirties, Will had met Baldwin in the Albert Hall and the fascinating conversation they had had on that occasion.

The Bill *had* to be a success and Gibley was grimly conscious that any hope of his continuing as the M.P. for the Rossford Constituency depended largely on the Press reception which his speech evoked.

At the week-end he contacted Jackie Mulholland of the *Gazette* and advised him confidentially about the alarming facts which he would be revealing in his speech supporting the Bill. Jackie seemed to be impressed with the story about how the Americans were peddling the chemical all over the world and yet not using it in their own country. He saw the basis of a good story and said that he would see the Editor about the possibility of the paper financing a special visit to London when the Bill came up.

Gibley offered to do what he could to get Jackie into the Press Gallery for the debate, but it seemed that the young reporter had a good number of friends in the Lobby and could arrange this himself. Had Gibley mentioned this American point to the Lobby boys? Not a word, Gibley assured him, and Jackie thought with pleasure how he would be a step ahead of the others. As the paper came out on a Tuesday, he would have time to write up a splendid story after the Friday debate and have a grand banner headline with a great story only a few days after the nationals would have covered it. And he would also be able to say that the *Gazette* reporter had known all about this shocking story for weeks, as they had been privileged to have an 'exclusive interview with Mr Horn'.

Gibley had every reason to be satisfied. But this was just too good to last and the bombshell dropped when

Gibley opened his mail on the Wednesday following and found in it a Circular Letter from the Agriculture Protection Association which had been addressed to all Members of Parliament.

Under the heading 'SPOTTED HUMMERFLY PROTECTION BILL—A THREAT TO AGRI-CULTURAL PROSPERITY', the Circular proceeded to explain how very vital BX20 insecticides were to farmers and how the banning of this chemical would have the same effect as the plague of locusts had on Pharaoh's cornfields. The Circular made it clear that, if the M.P.s of the country areas did not take every possible step to stop the Bill's progress, then the farming community would show even less enthusiasm to assist the Members at the next election than Moses and Aaron had shown when Pharaoh asked them to get him out of his trouble.

This was tragic. These country Members were terrified of the farmers and their votes. And if any measure attracted even the remotest criticism from the friends of farmers, at least 150 M.P.s would be instantly willing to demonstrate in Trafalgar Square and assure the world that freedom and democracy were at risk.

When Gibley tried to seek the support of one or two Members that day he found that the tolerance and understanding which he had found to date had been replaced with a sudden desire in almost every one to rush off to a pressing and urgent engagement. It was true that there was a quite substantial band of M.P.s of both Parties who, on a free vote, could be counted on to support anything which was disliked by the farmers. But the trouble was that their feelings were not strong enough to make them stay on in the House until 4 p.m. on a Friday while the farmer boys, anxious to have their names marked down on the side of the just in Hansard where it could be viewed by their local N.F.U. committees, would make the effort to be in their places.

As the days went by Gibley Horn saw his band of supporters shrinking and he decided that a blast of fire must come from those who were on his side. He contacted his ally, Miss Phillimore, who had by now received a copy of the A.P.A. Circular, and advised her that every M.P. must receive an equally stirring message from the Friendship League. Miss Phillimore's ire had been raised and she offered gallantly to write a letter condemning farmers and all they stood for and protesting violently against the enormous subsidies which they received and misused so blatantly in the destruction of the insect world. But Gibley explained patiently that a vitriolic attack on farmers would not entirely answer the demands of the situation—what was needed was a carefully argued and reasonable case for supporting the Bill.

This, Miss Phillimore assured him, could just as easily be done. And within forty-eight hours, the 630 Members of Parliament, from the Prime Minister to the humblest backbencher, received a stirring letter from the Executive Secretary of the Insect Friendship League.

'I implore you to give your active support to Mr Gibley Horn and his worthy colleagues who are promoting the Spotted Hummerfly Protection Bill. The evil shadow of science hangs over the cornfields of *your* constituency' ('Haven't even a blade of grass in mine,' Terry Lester had exclaimed at this) 'and chemical insecticides are threatening to condemn the insect world to extinction and a horrible death.

'We bring to your attention the noble Spotted Hummerfly, whose carefree existence is being snuffed out by BX20, the latest potion to escape from the laboratories of death. The Hummerfly causes no harm to man or crop.

NO CASE HAS BEEN ADVANCED THAT IT HARMS CROPS IN ANY WAY! AND YET IT SEEMS THAT FARMERS HAVE DECREED THAT IT MUST BE WIPED OFF THE FACE OF THE EARTH.

Stop this slaughter! Support the Bill now!'

With these stirring sentiments the Circular ended and poor Gibley realised that this kind of stuff would not cut much ice with his colleagues. If some big pressure group like the Unions or the Chamber of Commerce or the local councils could be persuaded that BX20 would affect their interests, it might be easier to mould the opinions of Members in favour of the Bill. But the little League had no such pulling power. And the important arguments about 'falling fever' had been left out on Gibley's instructions as he intended to keep this up his sleeve as a punch-line to persuade the waverers during the debate.

But Miss Phillimore had been busy in other directions.

She had sent circulars to the League's subscribers and 280 or so of them got out their pens and pencils and sent a flood of letters to their M.P.s. James Grattonby who received three such letters from his London Constituency came to the conclusion that the votes of three households, in a constituency with a majority of 29, could be significant and he advised the writers and Gibley Horn that he would fight to the death to save the Spotted Hummerfly.

But there were not many James Grattonbys in the House and not many constituencies with a majority of 29, and Gibley began to get a little depressed about the prospects for his Bill. The whole thing, he realised, would hinge on his speech and on the dramatic effect of the revelations which he was going to make. He thought of the great figures dotted over the history of Parliament and knew that he, like them, would rise to the occasion when the time came.

He had to harness every possible weapon in favour of his case and deploy all his forces. A letter from a Minister was always a help and so he got Mrs Milligan to send a letter to the Minister of Health enclosing the Press cuttings and asking what information the Minister could find out about 'falling fever' and any possible connection it might have with a chemical known as BX20.

✳✳✳   ✳✳✳   ✳✳✳

The snow was falling on the pavements of the Elephant and Castle on this early January day when, in the Ministry of Health, Albert A. Allenby looked out of the window of the room in which his desk was located and was not pleased with the world which he saw outside. A messy place, he thought. The Deputy Secretary had just popped into the room and given him a letter from some Scottish M.P. and instructed him to get weaving. There were a few suggestions as to how he could check up on the factual information referred to in the letter. But Albert knew, with the certainty of night and day, that the Deputy would chop to ribbons whatever letter he drafted, however splendid it was, just to impress upon him once again that it would be some considerable time before he attained the high standard of performance which was required in the Ministry of Health.

'Might have been all right in Department of Economic Affairs,' the Deputy would rasp out, 'but our letters have to be beyond reproach and never say anything which cannot be defended, without question, by the Minister in the House.'

But the Deputy had an unreasonably jaundiced view of Allenby's old Ministry. It had been a good set-up with plenty of bright sparks in it. And if it had been folded up when the new crowd took over this did not mean that the whole department had been a wash-out. If there were any defects, it had certainly not been the responsibility of Albert A. Allenby as the Deputy seemed to imply every time the subject was raised.

He didn't like working with this crowd. Felt like a musty old clerk, whereas in the old Ministry he had considered himself to be one of the new élite of whiz-kids.

What did this old Highlander want to know anyway? Did insecticides make farm workers fall over in a stupor? Probably they had been consuming too much cider!

'Check up with official records' he saw written on the paper. 'Phone Dr Connelly at Extension 285! Phone Mr Gates at the Chemical Institute. Contact Paraguay Embassy.' All this for one miserable letter!

What a wretched job! But he saw that it was 9.45 a.m. and there was the happy prospect of tea in view. So he addressed himself to the task.

*** *** ***

When, following an uneasy Christmas Recess and an increasingly anxious couple of weeks following the reassembly of Parliament, Gibley arrived down at London on 14th February, he was acutely conscious of the importance of the coming week in his life. This was to be 'make or break' week and he was not entirely happy at the prospect. Such confidence as he had shown in the past had been eaten into by the series of disasters which he had suffered in the recent weeks before Christmas. Major Perkins had telephoned repeatedly throughout the Recess and had been on again at the week-end to ask if Gibley had found time to 'reflect' and, when Gibley continued to assure him that a decision of this magnitude would require much more time, the Major had hinted darkly that his patience and that of the Executive Committee was not inexhaustible. They would, he added, be having the

Constituency A.G.M. in March and the workers would want to know where they stood.

This state of tension made it the more important for him to have a success on Friday and he therefore gave his whole attention to the speech which he would have to make. He busied himself in pressurising James Grattonby, John Knox-Crichton and David Forbes to make speeches or, at least, to ensure that the right noises of support were made at the appropriate time.

He was a little heartened too at the letter which he received from the Minister of Health. He knew that Ministers could not be definite about anything in letters, but the fact that the letter had not thrown his theory out of the window was encouraging to say the least. If the letter drafted by Albert Allenby had not been amended, the theory would indeed have hovered perilously near the brink because he had suggested that the Minister should end with the clear sentence that 'On the information I have there is no ground whatsoever for thinking that there is any direct connection between the outbreaks of 'falling fever' and the use of BX20 insecticides.'

But the Deputy Secretary, conscious that Gibley might possibly (although the chances were remote) have testimony from some medical authority that a prima facie case linking the two could be held to exist, had substituted the less definite pronouncement.

'While it is true that the medical authorities here and in Paraguay have not discovered any specific cause of this unfortunate malady known as 'falling

8

fever', the evidence linking the disease with BX20 insecticides is largely circumstantial and not of sufficient weight to justify any definite opinion being arrived at by my Ministry.'

There was an implication here, it seemed to Gibley, that the Ministry thought that there might be a link and that the only thing holding them back from making a definite pronouncement was the lack of specific evidence.

He felt more confident in facing the Commons now that he had a letter from the Ministry stating clearly that his theory might possibly have some foundation. He would, however, have been less confident if he had been aware of the fact that in one of the more remote Committee Rooms the officials of the Agriculture Protection Association were imparting to a number of his colleagues the most interesting information they had obtained regarding the Insect Friendship League and its worthy office-bearers.

✻✻✻   ✻✻✻   ✻✻✻

On the Thursday prior to the Debate, Jackie Mulholland and the *Gazette* reporter, arrived down at the House of Commons and Gibley entertained him to a drink. Jackie was enjoying his visit enormously, although he was conscious, all the time, that the Editor had insisted that a big story must be forthcoming to justify the substantial sum which the paper was expending on his London trip. But Jackie shared Gibley's enthusiasm and confidence and he took the liberty of tipping off some of the people he had met in the Lobby canteen that there was a very big story indeed to emerge under the rather unusual cover of the Spotted Hummerfly Protection Bill. So persuasive was he that some of the Lobby Correspondents decided that instead of staying away from the building on Friday and depending on the Agency tapes for their newspapers they would make a point of being there in person.

Gibley did not sleep a great deal that Thursday night and he looked again and again at the carefully prepared speech, notes of which he guarded as though it was a bar of fine gold. He was considerably heartened to receive, just before he entered the Chamber, a number of telegrams of support. One was from Margaret. Another from 'The President and Office Bearers of the I.F.L.' and a third from some unknown called 'J. Smith' who, from Bristol, had taken the trouble to send the message 'Protect Innocent Insects'. Probably a member of the Society whose enthusiasm had run away with him.

He was pleased to see on the benches that James Grattonby, Knox-Crichton and young Forbes were all in their places. Even old Will Francis had put in an appearance and was sitting there staring at a copy of the Bill, clearly wondering how on earth his name had got there.

After prayers were over and a tedious statement about meat imports had been made, Gibley was called upon to make his proposing speech. As he rose he suddenly thought how funny the whole thing was.

There was a big crowd of Members, all of whom were staying there to discuss a Bill which unimportant Gibley Horn had put forward. What in earth would have happened to them if he had decided to take a day off? Or if he had had a sudden attack of 'flu? But these things never seemed to happen. There were the Hansard Reporters sitting with pencils poised ready to take down his comments. This speech would go into the House of Commons records and could never be erased. Perhaps some M.P., two hundred years from now, would look through the archives and stumble on the proof of Gibley's immortality. And if Knox-Crichton interrupted his speech to say even a humble 'Hear, hear', that too would be recorded and available for the inspection of that chap who would not be born for at least 150 years. Quite a thought!

But he had to begin. The fight was on.

'Mr Speaker,' he read carefully from his notes. 'The Bill which I am introducing is rather an unusual one.'

('Hear, hear,' cried someone from the Opposition benches.)

'Because Private Member's Bill are customarily used to redress some grievance affecting people or some anomaly of the law. At first sight it would appear that the only people who would benefit from my Bill, if it were passed, are millions of little creatures known as Spotted Hummerflies who eke out their existence in the cornfields of our land.' Gibley had by now aroused the interest of the eighty or so Members who were present and also their curiosity.

'These insects used to exist in even greater numbers

but they are slowly being wiped out by a chemical insecticide known as BX20. If my Bill is passed it will be virtually impossible to use that insecticide in Britain and this, I hope to persuade you, would be a sensible and reasonable step to take.'

'Nonsense!' cried one county M.P. who clearly had many farmer constituents who thought differently. This was the first open show of hostility, but Gibley persevered.

'BX20 is manufactured in the United States, but at present is only used in some South American countries and in certain European ones. I will return to the significance of this point later,' he advised, to warn the audience that bigger shocks were in store for them.

He then proceeded to mention the facts and figures which he had obtained in Questions to the Ministries and pointed out that a considerable expenditure of foreign currency was involved.

'All to eradicate Spotted Hummerflies and some other insects of a similar type.'

He then went on to say something about the Hummerfly, this information having been gleaned from the Professor's Presidential Address, and explained that the little creatures did no harm to anyone.

The use of chemical insecticides had been causing concern over the years, he proceeded to expand his case. He then quoted, at length, from two books he had found in the Library which suggested that food produced from cereals treated with certain types of insecticides built up poisons within human bodies and could have long-term consequences which were not immediately apparent.

'These experts' (Gibley thought that it was safe to give them this title) 'have not been listened to by the world, in the absence of any specific information which could show that their fears were justified. But in the case of BX20 there are indications that troubles are appearing.' This contention with the obvious indication that proof was forthcoming made a number of M.P.s sit up and listen more carefully to what the old boy had to say.

Gibley then read out the reports about 'falling fever' and got a few laughs when he described the plight of the father of three who had fallen into a water trough. The extracts from the letter which he had received from the Minister of Health demonstrated clearly that the Ministry had not shut their eyes to the possibility that there might be something in this.

'Would the Hon. Member give way?' Malcolm Nixon-Plunkett, a farmers' champion, was on his feet and was indicating in the customary manner that he was anxious to ask Gibley a question. Gibley courteously gave way.

'Would my Hon. Friend agree that there is not one shred of specific evidence to link BX20 with "falling fever" and has he considered the possibility that the disease might be the result of handling certain of the newer types of chemical-based paints on agricultural implements and machines?'

Gibley had to admit that this possibility had not received his earnest consideration. But he claimed that there were more grounds to link the outbreak to BX20 than to some unspecified paint. Ridiculous idea, he thought.

Now he was building up to his punch-line. He had five pages of carefully-written oratory in which, without actually accusing the United States Government of being murderers and rogues, he had included several inferences that all was not well with the moral fibre and integrity of those moulding the destinies of that great nation. This was the real punchy stuff. And he hoped that the Press would lap it up.

He started the passage with appropriate seriousness.

'If we accept, and I think personally that there are sound reasons for believing that it is the case, that this chemical which was introduced only a few years ago, has harmful effects on human beings and produces a disease which has puzzled medical authorities all over the world, one question stands out.

'Why is it the case that this new chemical produced in the United States, distributed from the United States and originally discovered in the United States, is not in fact used by that nation?' He paused to let the point sink in; and, up in the Gallery, Jackie Mulholland started to scribble, furiously winking at some of the other reporters to let them know that the bomb was about to drop.

Nixon-Plunkett was on his feet again and Gibley was rather annoyed to be interrupted just at the beginning of his momentous accusation. But, having dealt adequately with him the last time, he decided to give way once again.

'While I have no idea what my Hon. Friend is driving at, is he not aware that it would be rather foolish for any United States farmers to use BX20 insecticides on account of the fact that insects of the oenfilia strain, which include Spotted Hummerflies, are not found in the United States?'

Gibley was fixed to his seat. Surely, he thought, those idiots in the League would have checked up on that obvious point. Surely they hadn't ditched him thoroughly in the soup? Why hadn't he thought about asking somebody about this? Of course he had meant to write to the American Embassy, but someone had said this would give the game away. How could he get out of this one? Why was fate always against him?

But he could not run away. He could not cry. He could not hide from himself the fact that Nixon-Plunkett's question had to be answered and he would then have to go on with his speech.

How he *hated* the whole crowd of them. And the whole wretched place! He would be glad to get out of it whether it was the result of Major Perkin's boot or not.

'That may be so,' Gibley stammered, 'but the whole thing is still surprising.' This poor effort at a recovery produced only a few titters followed by an embarrassed silence.

The next five pages of his speech would now have to be scrubbed, and Gibley realised to his horror that having only spoken for eight and a half minutes he now had only three pages to go. But where to start? He looked anxiously down page sixteen of his speech.

'In light of this inexplicable position,' he began.

'What inexplicable position?' questioned Nixon-Plunkett, clearly indicating his wonder whether Gibley was still referring to BX20 not being used in America or simply to the confusion which was obviously operating in the space between Gibley's large ears.

Gibley had indeed been referring to the American position, because this part of his speech followed on from his alarming accusations. But he decided just to continue, even although the splendid confidence and correct delivery of the beginning of his speech had quite disappeared.

'Members will wonder why we permit BX20 to be used in Britain without any control or further investigation. If it can be proved beyond a shadow of a doubt that the chemical does not have the harmful effects which I suggest,' he stumbled on, 'then we could reconsider the whole position later, but so long as the doubt remains it would be wise to ban the use of the chemical.'

'Votes for Hummerflies!' shouted one jolly Labour Member sensing that the speech was about to collapse.

This produced a great bellow of laughter and allowed the House to escape temporarily from the embarrassment which all Members present felt at Gibley's sudden lapse. Why had the old boy thrown away part of his speech? Was he feeling a bit unwell? Gibley had intended to follow up with a moving passage about the need to protect housewives and the effect which the chemical insecticides had on food. He even had a telling quotation from the Lady Chairman of the Housewives Action Committee, who had said recently that the way things were going, housewives would be reduced to a diet of vitamin pills and that although this would be good for slimming, it would make life less interesting.

But he knew that, without the American business, his speech had only a fraction of the weight which he had intended. He also had the futile feeling that, if he recovered well from his confusion, this would simply be helping the Insect League people who had sold him down the river so completely.

So he just said in conclusion:

'I hope that the Members will think seriously about this Bill and give it a Second Reading.'

He sat down.

John Knox-Crichton said 'Hear, hear', because he was very sorry for poor old Gibley who had failed so disastrously in what he had obviously hoped would be a great success.

James Grattonby also grunted 'Hear, hear', because he wished to convince himself that the case for the Bill which he was committed to supporting was a bit better than Gibley's comments would lead him to believe.

Sir Andrew Mellin said 'Hear, hear', because he thought that Nixon-Plunkett was an obnoxious little twerp and he didn't like the way he had treated Gibley.

And now the debate was open.

Several Members rose to their feet, but the Speaker's pleasure fell on Nixon-Plunkett who had clearly taken upon himself the opposition to the Bill.

'While we all appreciate the sincerity with which my Hon. Friend has advanced his argument'—this was the usual Parliamentary way of saying that the gentleman concerned was completely lacking in sense and sound argument—'I feel obliged to advise the House to oppose the Bill.'

He was, said Nixon-Plunkett, proud to represent a very fine constituency in a very fine county. It had the finest land and the finest farmers that ever were. And he had the highest opinion of all these fine farmers. And the farmers had lived up to the highest traditions of their noble trade by harnessing all the forces of science to the natural forces to ensure that British folk got the finest food that could be found in the world.

This was too much for Sir Andrew Mellin who, apart from disliking the young twerp, hated such an obvious display of crawling to a constituency.

'I hope,' he interjected with deep sarcasm, 'my Hon. Friend will reject his customary humility and take steps to ensure that his words are published in his local paper so that the fine farmers can know how their efforts are recognised.'

Blushing scarlet, but not to be diverted, Nixon-Plunkett plunged on:

'Anything which would adversely affect the interests of agriculture and its further development must be opposed by all those who have the great industry's welfare at heart,' he continued. This again would show the honest farmers in his Constituency what an excellent champion they had.

'I believe,' his voice slowed portentiously, 'that this Bill is one such measure because the effect of banning BX20 would be that the tikkinit as well as the relatively harmless Hummerfly would survive in increasing numbers, and all Hon. Members will be aware of the grave damage which the tikkinit can cause in grain fields.' Not many Members were aware of this, but Nixon-Plunkett looked so certain that most were prepared to give him the benefit of the doubt.

'But was the Spotted Hummerfly really so harmless?' Nixon-Plunkett asked. They were all aware of the terrible disease called 'hoof blight' which raged through the countryside from time to time and which resulted in many fine herds of cattle and thousands of pigs having to be slaughtered. Nobody was quite sure how the disease was spread because the normal precautions imposed by the Minister appeared to be ineffective in isolating the disease. It was noticeable that many of the major outbreaks had occurred in areas where Spotted Hummerflies abounded. Was it not possible that the Hummerflies were the secret bearers of this evil disease? At least there was as much reason to believe that the Hummerflies were responsible for 'hoof blight' as to believe that BX20 caused 'falling fever'.

Having made this telling point, Nixon-Plunkett moved on to the climax of his address.

He had received, he advised the House, a letter from the Insect Friendship League. He believed that most M.P.s had been privileged to have such a letter. The League was known to be behind the Bill and although he would not for a minute suggest that his Honourable Friend, the Member for Rossford, had simply picked up a Bill which had been written for him by an outside body, there was every reason for thinking that the League had a very large finger in this particular pie.

The President of the League was the only scientific

man on the Executive of the organisation. Professor Agrario Himmelstein was his name. But where was he a Professor? An inquiry at the League's offices had disclosed that the Professor was from Hungary (so that was who phoned, thought Miss Phillimore in the gallery), but he had been unable to ascertain whether the Professor's subject was science or in some other academic field. A chance meeting, however, with some Hungarians in London (by chance meeting he meant seven days of diligent research by officials of the Agriculture Protection Association) had disclosed that Professor Himmelstein was a Professor only in his own mind and that his sole claim to fame in the world of science was the fact that he had been employed, for six weeks, as a lens polisher at the Observatory at Carozkow, after which he had been dismissed for falling asleep on the job.

At this point there was a disturbance in the Gallery and a shout of 'Lies' rang out. A small figure with a white beard could be seen being escorted, protesting all the way, out of the Gallery.

In these circumstances, Nixon-Plunkett suggested without being the slightest put out by the row above him, it might be unwise to place too much significance on the scientific arguments advanced by the League.

He sat down, aware that he had demolished the case for the Bill. More than that. He had demolished its promoter who looked terribly alone and forlorn in his usual seat in the House. Gibley would have liked to flee, but it would seem very ungracious to depart when his own Bill was being discussed.

As the debate proceeded, Gibley was surprised to see that the next speaker from the Opposition side was none other than Pete McGarrity. Annoyed considerably by the young English twit who had made mincemeat of old Gibley, he came in with one of his very few speeches and, after saying some uncontroversial things about housewives and their natural abhorrence of chemically treated food, complimented Gibley on presenting the Bill so well. It was a noble, kindly gesture, but obviously designed to be just that.

The rest of the debate was taken up by several Members saying what fine farms were also in their constituencies and what solid upright chaps the farmers were and by an uproarious speech from James Grattonby who took the opportunity to read out the letters which he had received from three ladies in his constituency. These letters provided great amusement for the M.P.s, but Grattonby knew that the old dears would be thrilled to receive copies of Hansard with extracts of their letters contained therein and he trusted that they would show the document to at least twenty-nine of their friends and so double his slender majority.

When the vote came, a solid phalanx of county Members poured into the Noes Lobby and, with James Grattonby and David Forbes acting as tellers, Gibley had only seven supporters coming into the Ayes Lobby with him. There was Pete McGarrity, Sir Andrew Mellin, John Knox-Crichton, old Will Francis and three Liberals who, seeing David Forbes at the door, assumed that the Liberals must be in favour of the measure.

After it was over, Gibley stumbled out to the Lobby and, he was sure, to a life sentence of ridicule and humiliation. This was really the end! It was doubtful if any of the papers would cover the debate and those which did would laugh him out of court. Why on earth had he bothered with this silly mob of idiots at the Insect League? Why, in fact, had he been born at all?

※※※   ※※※   ※※※

Up in the Gallery, Jackie Mulholland was almost speechless with rage and embarrassment. To think that he had actually persuaded some Lobby correspondents, the kingpins of his profession, to go out of their way to report this tripe. And to think that this idiot of an M.P. had decided to put across this stuff about the Americans without even bothering to check up *why* the Americans did not use the insecticide. How on earth was he going to persuade the Editor that his journey had not been wasted? The fault was entirely Gibley's, but the Editor would probably think that he too should have probed a little deeper.

Then he suddenly had a thought. He *would* give the Editor a story. A real banner headline story! And, as the thought went round his narrow head, he could hardly wait to get to his typewriter.

※※※   ※※※   ※※※

Gibley had arranged to meet the League's Committee in the Lobby after the debate, but the 'Professor' was probably by now locked up, where he should have been years ago; and the other members of the Committee would be in no spirit to have a chat. So instead he went to the phone and called home.

'How did it go, Gibley?' asked Margaret anxiously. She feared the worst because, when she heard Gibley mentioning all this cloak-and-dagger stuff about the Americans spreading germs, she had a shrewd suspicion that her husband was a little out of his depth. He was always so enthusiastic before the event. And so remorseful afterwards.

'Pretty terrible,' he admitted. 'These Insect League people gave me a load of 'duff gen.' The only reason the chemicals are not used in America is because they have no Hummerflies there! They really let me down.'

As usual, Gibley was looking for sympathy after his latest disaster, but Margaret had the feeling that it was she, above all, who needed a little sympathy for having married such an idiot. If there was another story like the last one in the papers, she didn't know how she could possibly face the ladies at the shops. It was bad enough already and she had gone without sugar for two days because she could not bring herself to go down to the grocers.

The urgency in Gibley's voice, however, seemed to indicate that his depression was greater than usual; so Margaret, loyal as ever, felt obliged to ask him when he was coming home so that she could have a nice meal ready. He was really pitiful in one of these moods.

'Not coming home,' he said sulkily. 'Go and get a taxi down to the Airport and fly down for the week-end. I'll tell the hotel people you're coming. It'll be a break for you after all this publicity.'

It was a nice thought but Gibley was, to tell the truth, rather fearful of appearing in Rossford at the week-end in case the Press had another crack at him in the interim. The thought of another conversation with Major Perkins was just too much.

To Margaret, however, this was one of the soundest ideas Gibley had had for a long time. The thought of a trip to London was stimulating at all times, but the prospect of disappearing in the anonymous mass of the Metropolis was an even greater attraction. She felt very vulnerable at home and was quite convinced that all the clusters of people in the High Street had met together specifically to talk about her husband's latest bloomer.

'But what about the expense?' she asked.

'Blow the expense,' came the confident assurance from her improvident husband. 'We'll be able to save like mad during the Recess.'

And so Margaret decided to come down to London and was in the great city by 9 p.m. that night.

But, in the meantime, Gibley was alone with his worries. What an idiot he was! And he was nearing sixty now. Not only had he made a real mess of things in Parliament and missed all the opportunities which ten years provided, but he was on the point of being thrown out as an abysmal failure. There wasn't much time left for him in this life. One foot in the grave and the other skating on thin ice. And what high hopes he had had when he first came into Parliament. It had seemed to provide a chance to make a real hit after a business career marked neither by success nor achievement. And he had muffed it.

He felt a little better to have Margaret with him and he thought that the week-end would provide an opportunity for them to plan, as best they could, what little future life held in store for them.

Next morning, before eight o'clock struck, Gibley rushed out to buy every morning paper he could find. The popular papers appeared to have ignored the Bill entirely and the 'qualities' only had a small coverage in which the principal story was the suggestion by Nixon-Plunkett that 'hoof blight' might be spread by Spotted Hummerflies. One paper even went so far as to put in his photograph. It was Nixon-Plunkett who had stolen the show.

The Commentator had a cruel little report on the day's proceedings which included a complicated joke which endeavoured to associate the mysterious 'falling fever' disease with the poor performance put up by the Rossford M.P.

But, by and large, the whole thing was reported in a minor key and with little to draw attention to the fact that Parliament had met at all the previous day.

The week-end of Margaret's visit was quiet and pleasant. Gibley suddenly realised what a good life an M.P. could have, if he didn't have to bother about constituencies and elections and things like that. It must be great, he reflected, to be an M.P. in one of these African countries where they had no elections or else just one Party and one candidate to vote for. He was genuinely sorry when Sunday evening came and Margaret had to leave for home. There was nothing for her to go back to apart from a big, empty house. But there were, as she said, lots of little things to do about the house and the daily-help would be coming in on Monday.

But the next week was a terrible one for Gibley. Everyone knew about his Bill and his disastrous showing. They never forgot these things in Parliament. Look at that young fellow who made a bit of a boob when asking the Prime Minister a Question, eighteen months ago. He had tried to make a joke about the Security Services, at the Prime Minister's expense, and had asked Sir Oliver if he would tell his officials that walls have ears.

'My officials are well aware of the fact that walls have ears,' Sir Oliver had replied haughtily, 'and they are most careful with those, like the Honourable Member's, that are still a little wet at the back.' Terribly tedious patter when you read it in print, but the House had rocked at this one and the poor young fellow was greeted with a chorus of 'wet ears' whenever he rose to speak on any subject. And so it would be with Gibley. They would never forget.

As the following week dragged miserably by, Gibley decided that he had had quite enough. He would contact the Major at the week-end and tell him so. At the coming A.G.M. they could start to find some other bloke to carry the can in the next election. One name which would certainly not be on the ballot paper was that of Gibley Horn. He would make no more speeches, ask no more questions, get into no more trouble. And he would save like mad for the deposit on that little Highland hotel where he and Margaret would retire. They could keep Westminster with all its corridors of power and its hearts of stone. Gibley was getting out of this dump once and for all.

When he arrived at 'Beechgrove' on Friday he put through a telephone call to the Major. It was Mrs Perkins who answered; and she seemed distinctly hostile when she heard who the caller was.

'The Major's up North on business,' she explained. The fishing season was beginning in earnest and Gibley wondered what business could be conducted from a rowing boat at Loch Longany.

'Perhaps I could phone him next week-end?' he asked politely.

'He'll be home by then. I'll tell him you called, Mr Horn. Good morning.' The conversation was at an end.

'Well, Margaret,' he said, 'the die is cast and all that. I'll hand in my chips next week-end and we'll save like mad for the rest of the time I'm in the House.'

When Gibley had settled down, Margaret thought that it was safe to let him see the *Rossford Gazette* which, in its own words, went into every second Rossford home.

Gibley read the banner headline.

'THE SPOTTED HUMMERFLY SCANDAL'

'Our Member of Parliament in Rossford, Mr Gibley Horn,' the story continued, 'told Parliament on Friday about the Spotted Hummerfly Scandal. The *Gazette* agrees that it was a scandal, but not in the sense that Mr Horn argued.'

'It is a scandal that, after ten years in the House of Commons representing a constituency with enormous problems, our M.P. should make use of a Private Bill opportunity to seek powers to protect Spotted Hummerflies, insignificant insects which are virtually unknown in Scotland and which certainly bring no jobs to Rossford.

'It is a scandal that our M.P. should put the case so badly that only seven M.P.s should vote for his Bill.

'It is a scandal that Mr Horn should be taken in by the crackpot Insect Friendship League which is headed by a bogus professor from Hungary.

'It is a scandal that Mr Horn should have sought to protect an insect that is believed by many to spread hoof blight which causes such devastation on British farms.

'It is a scandal that Rossford's good name should be associated with such a silly and pointless exercise. Rossford has become the laughing stock of Parliament.

'The scandal must be stopped through the ballot box.'

Jackie Mulholland had gone to town, Gibley thought. Well, at least his journey to London had not been wasted. The Editor had got his story.

He was more than ever convinced that his decision

to telephone the Major and hand in his cards was the right one. And he resolved to start looking in the papers for any Highland hotels advertised for sale. If the election came next year, he would have to be quick off the mark.

In his present frame of mind he decided he would not go down to London unless it was absolutely necessary. But there was a vote at half past three on Monday and so this week at least he would have to go down as usual. He was not a man to let people down.

✳✳✳　✳✳✳　✳✳✳

When he arrived in London Gibley resolved that, instead of rushing in to cope with his mail, he would leave it till the next day, so he spent the morning wandering around the shops and thoroughly enjoying himself. He decided to have lunch away from Parliament and amused himself hugely talking with some American tourists who came and sat at his table in the restaurant of one of the big stores.

Three o'clock his watch said. He would have to get moving as the vote was at three-thirty. So he strolled along to the Commons and entered the Members' Lobby as quietly and unostentatiously as was possible. No sooner had he appeared, however, than one of the Whips came rushing up to him in great agitation.

'Where on earth have you been? Your Question to the Minister of Science is on the Order Paper. The Minister wants to answer it specially at the end of Question Time. Better get in to the Chamber.'

What the blazes was the fellow talking about? thought Gibley. He wasn't going to put down any more Questions and he couldn't remember having put down any recently.

Then he remembered that silly question which Miss Phillimore asked him to put down about the representations which the League had made to the Minister of Science. Well, he certainly wasn't going to ask this one.

'I'll just let that Question drop,' said Gibley. 'What's all the fuss about anyway. Lots of Members miss Questions and nobody bothers about it.'

But the Whip was adamant. 'The Minister has *specially* arranged to answer this one at the end of Question Time. He *must* have something important to say.'

There must be some mistake, thought Gibley. The Minister wouldn't bother about these silly Hummerfly people. And even if, by a strange miracle, it had turned out that BX20 was spreading death and destruction over the globe, there would be no need to answer a Question especially about it.

But the Whip was insistent and manoeuvred Gibley towards the door of the Chamber at the same time showing an Order Paper with all the Questions to be asked that day printed on it.

'Go and sit down,' the Whip implored. So Gibley went and sat down and listened to the Minister of Science, Sir Algernon Bootle, answering the questions. It was now 3.20 p.m and. the Minister was at Question 27. A quick look at the Order Paper showed Gibley that his Question was number 40 and would not normally have been reached before Question Time ended at 3.30. p.m.

Sir Algernon must be off his head to anwser a question about representations from the Insect League about the growth and treatment of cereal crops and the consequences which this would have on the population of the World. It was probably all a terrible mistake and nothing at all would happen at half past three.

Still, thought Gibley, I'd better get a supplementary question ready, just in case the question is answered. He could always ask the Minister what reports he had received from Paraguay on the matter. So he wrote down carefully at the top of his Order Paper, 'WHILE THANKING THE MINISTER FOR THAT INFORMATION WOULD HE PLEASE INDICATE WHAT RECENT REPORTS HE HAS RECEIVED FROM PARAGUAY ON THIS MATTER?' That would do. But the whole thing was a bit of a mystery.

Three-thirty struck. Gibley was astonished to sees Sir Algernon getting up at the Dispatch Box, putting on his most serious and statesmanlike look and announcing sonorously, 'With the permission of the House I should like now to answer Question 40 which is in the name of the Hon. Member for Rossford.'

He must be potty, Gibley thought, and looked again at his Question.

'Mr Gibley Horn (Rossford) to ask the Minister of Science what information he has received from the International Physics Laboratory . . .'

The what? No, it was the Insect Friendship League. Stop! Alarm! Gibley was in a panic. He wanted to tell the old fool that there had been a big mistake. Gibley had never heard of the International Physics Laboratory! He never wanted to either!

But Sir Algernon was ready to go. He had to be careful about this one because it was Big Time. His officials were astounded when the Question had appeared on the Order Paper, because every aspect of this cereal project had been kept completely secret and all the files were marked 'Top Secret', which indicated that the leaking of any of the contents would be a grave national tragedy. Someone must have spilled the beans. But who? And how? They had hoped to make an official announcement in May. But the Minister, anxious to avoid the danger of one of his backbenchers blurting out part of the news, decided to advance the official announcement to coincide with the Question.

To an attentive and packed House and to a panic-stricken Gibley, Sir Algernon began to unfold the tale:

'In answer to the Question I have to advise that, in conditions of the greatest secrecy, the International Physics Laboratory, which is entirely financed and controlled by her Majesty's Government, in conjunction with our own Space Research Division, have been engaged on a project to study the effect on cereal growth of exposure of the seeds to the atmosphere between 200 and 250 miles above the earth. This area is known to astronomers as the O'Brien Ring and our scientists have been aware, for some considerable time, that the atmosphere had some special features. It was discovered that cereal seeds sent up in a rocket, in a container made of a highly secret alloy, came back to earth possessing extraordinary powers of growth without any deterioration or reduction in the standard of the wheat grown.

'The best estimate I can give is that wheat grown from these seeds will produce about ten times the yield per acre of seeds planted in ideal conditions and with the maximum protection from insects or disease.

'The consequences of this for World food supplies is truly remarkable and I am conscious that I am making one of the most momentous announcements of the century and perhaps in the history of the human race.

'The most significant aspect of the whole matter is that the entire process and the formula of the alloy used in the container is entirely in British hands. Great praise is due to the scientists in the I.P.L. and in our Space Research venture for achieving this wonderful success.'

The House was astonished. Gibley was almost paralytic. His mind was a blank and, as he was called by the Speaker to ask his Supplementary, he could only mutter that while thanking the Minister for that information, would he please indicate what recent reports he had received from Paraguay?

The Minister was dumfounded. Then old Horn *must* know the whole story. How was this possible? Only he,

Sir Oliver and the President of Paraguay knew this.
The paper had only been signed yesterday. But he was
fortunately in a position to announce it officially.

'It had not been my intention to speak on this point,'
he advised Gibley gravely. 'But, as the Hon. Member
obviously is aware, the alloy used in the seed containers
requires quantities of a new metal which can be
obtained only from certain mines in Paraguay and I
have received a flash, only fifteen minutes ago, to say
that both Governments have ratified a Treaty of
Friendship and Co-operation which is to last for a
hundred years and which will ensure to Britain
adequate supplies of the metal for that period of time.'

The announcement was greeted with long and lusty
cheering because it was immediately obvious to all,
save poor old Gibley who was now only half-conscious,
that this was a fantastic new development which would
upset the whole balance of power in the world and put
Britain in the position of leadership from which she
had fallen such a long way in recent decades.

Gibley suddenly found himself being slapped on the
back by those around him as though he had fired off
the rockets himself. And, as he staggered out of the
Chamber, he was immediately grabbed by a host of
Lobby men who asked a series of garbled questions.
How had he known? Hadn't the Question been on the
Order Paper for over a fortnight? Had he been involved
in the secret negotiations? Had his Bill been a glorious
cover to confuse the enemy and let them think that our
only interest in Paraguay was Spotted Hummerflies?
How close was he to Sir Oliver?

But one burly man grabbed Gibley forcibly before these questions could be answered and asked him if he would do a television interview in five minutes which would be flashed all over the world by satellite.

And, before he had even thought about it, he found himself in front of a screen.

'When did you first know about this fantastic news, Mr Horn?'

A rather puzzled and scared Gibley who, the interviewer realised, must be apprehensive about giving away any state secrets, said:

'I put down the Question some weeks ago.'

'And how deeply involved were you in the negotiations between the Prime Minister and the President of Paraguay?'

Gibley was terrified. He felt that he was dropping into a bigger trough than even the Spotted Hummerfly disaster. So he said, simply, 'I can't speak for Sir Oliver.' And then, to play safe, 'He's a very great statesman.'

The interviewer was by now convinced that Gibley had been up to his eyes in the whole business. So he chanced a question which he knew would be delicate.

'But how was it possible to keep our interests in the new metal in Paraguay so secret and out of the hands of our enemies?'

Gibley didn't know what this was all about but the mention of Paraguay struck a bell.

'Perhaps you didn't hear my Speech in the House, I talked a lot about Paraguay. Told them all how worried we were about 'falling fever'. Breaking out all over the place there.'

'So your Bill was a cover to protect our national security and give others the impression that your interest was in insects and fevers? Quite brilliant! And you had to stand the ridicule of your own colleagues in the House in the process?' The interviewer laughed heartily and excitedly at this.

Gibley realised dimly that here was a possible excuse for his crashing failure on that awful Friday. He didn't quite grasp the significance. But he felt that it was safe to say, 'Well, you never know!'

The interview ended, and for the next few days millions of viewers, all over the world, were fascinated to see the pictures of the quiet little Member of Parliament who had somehow been deeply involved in this miraculous new British discovery which could solve the World's problem of hunger.

As he walked out of the House in a daze, Gibley was conscious of hundreds of flash bulbs popping and microphones being shoved into his face. The whole world seemed to have gone mad! He was pursued by reporters to his hotel and the manager had a hectic time fighting them off. He decided to phone the House and find out what was happening there and precisely the extent to which he was involved in it.

When he contacted the Whips' Office he was immediately put through to the Chief.

'Wonderful show, Gibley!' the great man said. 'Must tell me the whole story some time.'

'I'm being mobbed by reporters in the hotel,' Gibley shouted in desperation, but in delight to find how popular he was with the boss. 'Any chance of getting away home for a day or two?'

'Of course, of course, old boy. We'll fix up a pair till the end of the week. But, remember, I want to hear the *whole* story some day.'

Gibley, by now quite beside himself, fled out to the Airport, pursued by cars and vans loaded with reporters. When the staff there saw what a V.I.P. was in their midst, they took him away to a private room and rushed him by car to the next plane for Glasgow.

But word of Gibley's arrival reached Glasgow before him and there, at the airport, was a vast crowd of reporters. He had slept most of the journey, feeling quite exhausted and still unable to grasp the whole business. He was amazed to find that some of the public at the Airport, who had read their evening papers, were cheering him.

He took a taxi straight home while the television newsman was saying into a microphone that Gibley Horn, the mystery man in the corn miracle space project, was leaving now for his home in Rossford. When he arrived at 'Beechgrove' he was amazed to find a huge crowd outside the gate cheering lustily and singing, 'For he's a jolly good fellow'.

When he got to the door, confused and worn out, he was shattered to find Margaret throwing her arms around him and saying, between sobs, 'I'm so *proud* of you, dear. You were wonderful on television. And to think I never knew anything about it! No wonder you were so worried!'

Gibley helped himself to a large gin. He sat down. He pondered. He read the papers. He saw his interview when it was repeated for the sixth time on television. It dawned on him gradually what the whole thing was about. And while the telephone rang all the time, with Margaret answering, she asked him to come to only one call. It was from Major Perkins.

'Wonderful stuff, Gibley!' the Major shouted from the hotel by the lochside. 'Always knew you had it in you. We're all behind you old boy! I've told all the chaps up here that I'm the Chairman of Rossford Tories. They bought me drink after drink and actually sang—"For he's a jolly good fellow . . ." '

What was the real story behind this powerful mystery man's part in the Great Rocket Project?

The newspapers were to ask this question for years after the event.

But only one man knew. Sir Gibley Horn, M.P.

And he wasn't telling anybody!!